"This book literally had me crying. It was really good! . . . I would totally recommend this book!"
—Erin B., teenaged reviewer and book blogger, NetGalley

Aionios Books
Carlsbad, California

Praise for

DoWn in the BeLLY oF tHe whALe

"Bowles... clearly understands the world of young adults. Her depiction of Harper—her anxieties and excitability; her inner and outer personas; her heightened sense of the importance of "now"—cannot fail to pull readers into a teen mindset. The story is increasingly dark, yet in the telling it neither wallows nor depresses. Harper is allowed strength in her vulnerability. For all her isolation, it is her empathy that makes her special. There is a message here but not one that is pushed beyond the pale. Bowles writes to engage and to confront yet always seemingly with the intent to uplift. The resulting novel, far from being a leaden treatise on teen suffering, spurns literary pretensions and strives instead to include Harper's generation of young adults and give this group its due. Girls especially will relate, but there is room here for everyone. A sage, vivacious tale of people set apart and brought together."
—*Kirkus Reviews*

"Bowles' writing is lively and fun, yet still grounded and full of depth.... This is a wonderful book that cleverly explores some powerful and painful emotions."
—Victor Catano, best-selling author of *Tail & Trouble*

"Tackles sensitive social issues with heartfelt emotion and tender wit.... Well-drawn characters and themes exploring the mysterious power of the unseen infuse this inventive, revelatory novel."
—Kathleen Gerard, author of the novels *The Thing Is*, *In Transit*, and *Cold Comfort*

"I have lived through a trauma similar to one described in this book, and Kelley handles it in a careful, tactful, and compassionate manner. She illustrates good role models for healthy families as well as a gentle treatment of dysfunctional ones. . . . dense with activity and drama, dealing with difficult topics that are on a teenager's mind in a sensitive manner that includes a good dose of humor and healing."
—Laura H Kelly, author, contributor to the anthology, *Things We Haven't Said*

"An enjoyable and captivating read."
—Brian S. Leon, author of *Havoc Rising*

"Sometimes funny, sometimes sad, sometimes hopeful, always true . . . *Down in the Belly of the Whale* is *Ordinary People* for a new generation."
—Jason Parent, author of *What Hides Within* and *Seeing Evil*

"Humorous and harrowing, romantic and revealing, and an honest true-to-life lesson about being a teenager in this most interesting of times. . . . definitely a must read."
—Shawn Clingman, English/drama teacher and director, Grand Junction High School.

"A fast-paced, yet heartfelt account of an average teenager whose life takes a series of sudden and unexpected turns. . . . Possibly the most important aspect of *Down in the Belly of the Whale*, are the messages that it conveys. Some of these messages are to be brave, even when you think you cannot be, that you belong even when you think you do not, that the person you thought you loved is not the right person for you, and that high school anatomy is as awful as I has I remember it."
—Timmie Quitugua, librarian

Down in the Belly of the Whale

Kelley Kay Bowles

Down in the Belly of the Whale.
Copyright © 2018 by Kelley Kay Bowles. All rights reserved.
No part of this book may be used or reproduced in any manner without prior written permission from publisher except in the case of brief quotations embodied in critical articles or reviews.

For information, please address:
Aionios Books, LLC, P.O. Box 1010, Carlsbad, CA, 92018, USA.
AioniosBooks.com
Publisher@AioniosBooks.com

Scripture texts in this work are taken from the *New American Bible, revised edition* © 2010, 1991, 1986, 1970 Confraternity of Christian Doctrine, Washington, DC and are used by permission of the copyright owner. All Rights Reserved. No part of the *New American Bible* may be reproduced in any form without permission in writing from the copyright owner.

This book is a work of fiction. Names and characters are the product of the author's imagination. Any resemblance to actual persons, living or dead, or to actual events is coincidental.

Book design by Gerardeen M. Santiago

Published 2018, by Aionios Books, LLC.
Printed in the United States of America.
ISBN-13: 978-0-9980844-7-3 (Paperback)
Library of Congress Control Number: 2018932950

*This book is dedicated to my husband,
for his awe-inspiring support in this dream called Writer.
I love you, "Jim Dear." Thank you for your belief in me.*

You cast me into the deep, into the heart of the sea,
  and the flood enveloped me;
All your breakers and your billows
  passed over me.

—Jonah 2:4
New American Bible (Revised Edition)

CHaPTeRS

1. Outcast ---------------- 1
2. Anxiety ---------------- 9
3. Angst ------------------ 17
4. Daydream -------------- 23
5. Trickery --------------- 27
6. Ceaseless -------------- 33
7. Blur ------------------- 37
8. Dissection ------------ 43
9. Hives ------------------ 49
10. Flummoxed ----------- 55
11. Outsider -------------- 63
12. Abuse ----------------- 67
13. Test ------------------- 77
14. Voluminous ----------- 83
15. Rescue ---------------- 89
16. Outcry ---------------- 93
17. Fear ------------------ 101
18. Changeling ---------- 109
19. Prognosis ------------ 117
20. Overwhelmed ------- 123
21. Limbo ---------------- 131
22. Patience ------------- 137
23. Influence ------------ 145
24. Premature ----------- 151
25. Introduction -------- 157
26. Apprehension ------- 167
27. Usefulness ---------- 177
28. Trepidation --------- 183
29. Success -------------- 193
30. Relief ---------------- 199
31. Purpose ------------- 209

1. Outcast

outcast /out kast/ n. 1. A person who has been rejected by society or a social group.

∞∞∞

My latest theory is that I must be a changeling.

I've read myths about changelings in various books and encyclopedias. They have one basic thing in common: a changeling is a creature switched with a child at birth, because someone wants the child more than the creature. I think I am the creature, and I feel sorry for the kid who got switched, because these parents aren't too bad, usually.

Oh, and did I mention the creatures doing the switching are trolls?

The changeling child at first looks like the human it substitutes, but gradually grows worse in appearance and behavior: ugly, malformed, ill tempered, given to screaming and biting.

My baby pictures are pretty cute, all toothless smiles and fat rolls, but right now as a sophomore, I have a zit the size of Cleveland right in the middle of my chin, my chest is less than spectacular, and growing my kinky brown hair long does little

2

to affect its behavior, which means it always looks like mini tornadoes have set up camp in my follicles.

I hate over half of my teachers. I have no siblings and only one real friend.

Since society in general frowns upon screaming and biting, I kinda only do that alone and to a pillow. So I totally agree with the changeling definition.

🌀🌀🌀

"**Mizzes Harper Southwood!** Ciao, bella! And how are ah-we thees morning? Ah-rrravishing, I can see. May I have ah-thees dance?" And he grabs my arm to start twirling me around the kitchen like a rag doll. My feet trip across the hardwood as I try to follow his rhythm.

This is my Uncle Peter, who is the only person in my family to whom I could maybe be genetically linked. We call him Uncle Pasta, because he is short but still skinny and linguini lanky, if a short person can be such a thing. He also has tornado hair, which he keeps short enough for it to be called kinky.

Plus he has this trick he loves to pull out at holiday dinners: He shoves a piece of spaghetti up his nose and pulls it out of his mouth. Then he kind of yanks both ends back and forth —al dente spaghetti, I'm sure, because otherwise it would break.

What does "al dente" mean in its original language, do you suppose? Something about how chewy and gross it is on your dentals, maybe. I'll have to look it up. Anyway, he likes to talk in this pseudo-Italian accent, which is another reason for the nickname.

He lives in our basement, which is why he flounces into the kitchen, scaring the bejesus out of me, at the ungodly hour of timetogotoschool.

"Did I mention I have a date tonight?" he says, opening a

kitchen cabinet to pull out a cereal bowl. "An ab-so-lootlee scrumptious man named ah-Charles. I theenk he rrreally likes me, too."

"Oh, I'm sure he does, Uncle Pasta," says I. "You, also, are ravishing. Whatever are you going to wear?"

Uncle Pasta and I aren't genetically linked in the matter of sexual orientation. At least, I don't think we are, judging by the way my stomach takes a nosedive every time I hear the name Larson McCready, or God forbid I see him and he sees me with the zit and the hair and the increasingly troll-like features.

Uncle Pasta sounds like a big outlandish goofball when he sneaks up on me and flings me around, with the accent and the al dente tricks and all, but he's really sweet and mellow and kind of insecure, inside.

"I'm sure he really likes you, Uncle Peter. You're one of the loveliest people I know."

He kisses my cheek. "No, you are the loveliest person, Little Miss Lovely. I think I'm going to wear jeans and a button-up shirt. Nice but casual, you know?"

I kiss his cheek. "It's going to be great. You'll be awesome, I know."

Uncle Pasta sneezes, and my nose starts to twitch.

"Oh, be careful, though. I think you're catching a cold."

He looks at me. "I hope you're wrong this time. I'm off to drown in a quart of orange juice, just in case." He drops the cereal bowl on the counter to open the fridge.

Changeling stories don't say that changelings have any special powers, except that they are wiser than human children. Which is cool. It's something to hang on to when my hair explodes out of the ponytail or my dad's acting a little douchey. But I think my troll family might have had a strange quirk, a sense of some sort. When people around me are getting sick, my nose itches, or I start sneezing, or my body reacts in some bizarre way.

It's not a gift or a power in my opinion, because it doesn't do anything for anybody. I can warn people to dive into the orange juice, I guess, but aren't you supposed to drink that stuff a lot anyway? Some help I am. I have this recurring fantasy where I can actually SEE the germ or the bacterium or whatever, with my intensive X-ray vision, and then I spray some sort of supernatural mojo out my nose that transforms the offending germ into a super vitamin that makes you healthier.

It's a nice dream, but so is cascading hair or Larson McCready on speed dial, always answering his cell and dying to take me out on the town.

Uncle Pasta heads to the fridge with fingertips squeezing at his lymph nodes. I feel helpless, like always, but I guess all I can do right now is go to school.

ʕʘʔʕʘʔʕʘʔ

The street's deserted this morning, which is unusual. Normally there are these four elderly people, three women and a man, who traipse the sidewalk in a single-file line. They move their arms in sync: a slow-motion march where their elbows move from their waists up toward the sky and back at about negative ten miles per hour. I think they're doing some sort of strange *tai chi* for old people—I'll have to look it up.

I'm glad for the solitude: the half-mile walk to my high school gives me time to consider the best way to avoid troll-ish mishaps and embarrassing situations. Plus I need to rehearse what to say to my friend Cora Perkins. She's been acting really weird lately, and she makes the backs of my knees itch. Don't ask me why. We've been friends for the past year and she's never been sick, and besides, my knees? Whatever.

I spot her on a bench in the middle of the courtyard. Cora has this really cool hair that is the complete opposite of mine: blond and long and falls straight like a sheet, but today it's tied in a weird knot at the base of her skull and looks dirty. She's wearing jeans and a long-sleeved shirt, even though school has only been on for a week, and it's been about ninety-five degrees every day since it started. "Hey, you," I say. "Are you OK?"

Cora snorts and rolls her eyes. "Define 'OK.' I'm not sick, if that's what you mean, crazy changeling woman." She gives me a faint grin, which makes her look a little better, but still not her normal self.

Cora knows all about my suspicions of trollhood and the dry-mouth disease I am afflicted with around Larson, and she's a wicked good listener and caring friend. She still tells me nearly nothing about herself, though. I know her mom is dead and her dad is militaristic even though he's a plumber. I've met him a few times, but he seems like an afterthought in Cora's life—she ignores him when we're (rarely) at her house and spends all her free time at mine. Mostly she dodges questions about the way she feels and what's happening in her life, switching the subject over to me or telling these really dumb jokes.

"I'm fine," she says. "Hey, knock knock."

I sigh in frustration and my knee twitches, an invisible doctor tapping with a plexor. "Who's there?"

"Nobody."

"Nobody who?"

She's silent.

It takes me a second. "Oh, har har."

She smiles, a real one now, and I am once again surprised that someone as pretty and nice as she is wants to hang out with me, the troll. Her eyes are green and shaped like almonds, and guys watch her when she walks by, and you can tell they talk about her when she's gone.

The Preps AND the Jocks AND the Dramatics are always angling for Cora to join their respective groups, but she says she'd

rather not hang out with kids who could have been lobotomized extras in a teenage movie, and besides, she wants to be around people who will help keep her brain functioning. That's me, I guess, maybe because I'm always looking everything up.

"Did you do the paper for Carstead?" I ask.

Cora flings her hands skyward. "Awright, tell me this. How do we find symbolism in a poem that has . . . count 'em . . . sixteen words in it? And then write a one-thousand-word essay on the previously read sixteen-word poem?"

"I take it that's a no?"

"Oh no, I wrote it. I said something about the red wheelbarrow representing our firefighters, and it's glazed with water to put out the fire that is burning the white chickens that represent the Twin Towers on 9/11. I think it's so much baloney I can hardly stand it. But you know Carstead has such a jones for even an ah-TEM-pted analysis, I figured . . ."

I shrug. "Yep. At least she's not one of those who says you can only do it her way to get the *A*." I finger the zipper on my backpack, thinking about the essay. "I said something about how they are all such mundane items: rain, wheelbarrow, chickens, but so much depends on them because without the everyday stuff you can't appreciate something extraordinary."

She looks at me. "Harper, that's profound. No wonder you're like, Carstead's love child." She pats my back like I'm a puppy and I push her hand away because here come three basketball players—one of whom is Larson McCready.

Oh, no. I bet he would never say "one of whom," and I can feel some ponytail hair sticking out in ways the universe never intended hair to go.

One of the guys, Mike, says, "Hey Cora. Great shirt. It would look better on my floor, though."

Cora looks at him like a cow just flew out of his nose. "Hey, Mike. I think you would look better with your face under

my boot, but hey look—I'm wearing flip-flops. Must be your lucky day."

The other guys crack up and shove Mike down the walk, calling sayonara to Cora. Only to Cora.

Larson is bringing up the rear of the group. My nails dig into my palms in the effort to raise my hand for a wave, but nothing happens and his head's down and doesn't even swing my way. My fingertips slide up to cover the zit, but it doesn't matter—he's already gone.

Cora looks at me. "So when are you going to talk to him, chickadee?"

I move my hands down to my neck and can feel the heat blossoming there. "I don't know. Maybe when these hives stop spontaneously appearing whenever he comes within ten or twenty feet."

She leans over to pull at the neckline of my T-shirt. "Oh, yeah. Wow. I thought you only got hives when you were confronted with an authority figure."

I stand at the sound of the bell and we head for our first hour classes, which are unfortunately different. "Yes, that, and when I'm so mad I feel like my eyeballs will pop, oh, and don't forget the crying. The nervousness and the fear and the anger bring on the hives and the uncontrollable welling of tears, which is why I'm such an impressive specimen, don't you think?"

We walk together for as long as possible. Cora flings an arm around my shoulders. "You betcha," she grins. "I am totally and completely impressed."

"You know it."

2. ANXieTY

anxiety /aNG zīedē/ n. a feeling of worry, nervousness or unease, typically about an imminent event or something with an uncertain outcome.

◎◎◎

The hives fade as I head for my acting class, which I only signed up for so Cora and I could have an elective together, but then the stupid computer ignored her request and stuck her in Family Living, which I suppose could be cool if it had any discussions ACTUAL families could use.

Instead, according to Cora, it is taught by this little fat woman called Ms. Tooney, who has never been married or had any children and talks only about abstinence because that's the only condition she's ever been in her entire life. Probably through no choice of her own. Oh, and I guess she talks about checkbooks, like people even use those anymore.

So I am here in Acting 1 without Cora, with Miss Bakener, who is certifiably bonkers and today is making us do things to "appropriately utilize our space." This I guess means you cross the floor like your character. She demonstrates how a drunken has-been actress would do this.

She always wears these floral broomstick skirts with Birkenstocks, and she grabs the flowers in chunks to get the skirt out of the way while she weaves and staggers, her red hair seeming to tumble ahead of the rest of her body. She doesn't say anything or slur any words, because we can't start appropriately utilizing our voices until next week.

"OK!" Miss Bakener says brightly, flinging her arms wide from the middle of the stage. "Do you get it? Let's see . . . Cade Castell. Why don't you move across the floor like a soldier?"

Cade Castell is this super-smart Goth guy I've gone to school with since second grade. We never talk, but every now and then we share a look that seems to say, it's OK, we're in this together. I don't know why we do this.

He gives me that look now, and does a stiff, toy-soldier march: one, two (with a corresponding salute), one, two. It's a crack-up, because every time he raises his hand to his forehead I see him bringing up the glinting pewter skull ring on his middle finger to smartly touch off a hoop that graces the edge of his eyebrow. The long black hair that wiggles with his jerky motion just completes the picture. General Patton meets Dracula. Bakener seems to like it, though, so Cade's off the hook and he escapes back to the edge of the stage.

Bakener walks up to me and looks down at the list. "Let's see—Harper Southwood, right?"

I nod, and my hand flies to my chest to ward off the hives. Please, please don't give me anything hideous, like . . . I don't know. . . .

"Why don't YOU utilize your space like an overzealous beauty queen?" she grins.

OK, please don't give me the overzealous beauty queen. I guess she's putting our fledgling acting skills to the ultimate test by picking characters to whom we couldn't possibly relate. I don't have the slightest idea how to do an overzealous beauty queen, so I walk with large steps, swinging my head back and forth the way I imagine Marilyn Monroe would do it. A huge snicker from the back of the group halts the walk and swing and propels me across the rest of the stage lightning quick, like Charlie Chaplin. Why couldn't I be Charlie Chaplin?

"OK, Harper," says Miss Bakener. "Good effort."

This comment, near as I can tell, is teacher-speak for "that really sucked, but my job is to not fully decimate you, at least not right away."

I spend the rest of the class trying to avoid perpetuating more snickers, which is tough when you use words like "perpetuating" in casual conversation. But at least I didn't have to pretend to be something overzealous, which I'm really not.

I'm just glad Larson isn't in this class.

So I go to Algebra 3/4 and then PE and then Anatomy—AKA Can't Do Numbers No Matter How Hard I Try, More Humiliation, and God Help Me I'm Gonna Have to Dissect Cats in the Same Room as Larson, respectively.

First, math. I don't understand how I can get straight *A*'s in every class I've taken since kindergarten, but then you get me in a class that uses "theorems," and all I can do is pronounce and spell the word. Maybe trolls don't do numbers.

And PE has been the definition of shame and sorrow since the invention of dodgeball, but at least the teacher has to give you an *A* for merely having vital signs. Until high school. Here there are phys ed fanatics who pull out the stopwatch to time everything you do, and they give you a grade for how fast you do it.

My PE teacher is Ms. Haglione. She wears orange terrycloth shorts and knee socks straight out of 1972. Her yellow polo shirt has lapels about a foot wide, and a matching terry-cloth headband keeps her inch-high-shorn brown hair out of her eyeballs. She looks like a highlighter.

Today she pulls her humongous whistle out from under her shirt and blows to wake the dead. "OK, Pinewood High School Wildcats of second period!" she yells. "Today we test your mettle! You can throw your teacher-my-tummy-aches complaints out the window, because they won't weasel ya outta nothin' today. Today is your two-week anniversary of bein' a Wildcat, and we're celebrating with wind sprints and timed push-ups and sit-ups. Lllllet's roll!" The whistle screams again and the torture begins.

I feel terrible when this one girl named Allison collapses on her first push-up, and I think this one kid Danny is coming down with the chicken pox or something major, because I sneeze so violently with each and every one of his sit-ups that I have to move across the floor to do mine.

Ms. HAG-lione just stops her watch at the end of my hundred-yard dash and makes these little clicking noises while writing down the time. At least this was better than screaming "F! You FAIL at running, you pansy little Nancy girl!" which is kind of what I was expecting.

Anatomy, despite the hives I can't escape when I walk in there and see Larson, at least has a teacher I can appreciate. A little. His name is Mr. Wolfram, and anyone can see he's all about science. And Hawaiian shirts, which he wears even in winter. It's kind of . . . refreshing, I guess. Not the shirts but the love of the subject, and while I spend most of my time in there wishing Larson would look my way and terrified he might look my way, sometimes I just sit in class and hope I'll be able to find a passion for my work like Wolfram has.

ම‍ම‍ම

I breathe a big sigh of relief when time comes for Mrs. Carstead's Comp. 10 class. The last class of the day, a bastion of safety, not only because I come brandishing what I must say is a stellar display of wordplay on "The Red Wheelbarrow," whatever that poem is really about, but also because Cora is there.

Cora sits in our usual back row place, which is a standard seating requirement no matter how good the teacher might be. She's leaning back with one knee propped on the seat of the chair, a pant leg scrunched up to expose a pale calf. She picks at what looks like a pair of cross cuts, and when she looks up to catch my eye, pulls the pant leg down and sits up straight.

"What's the matter? Are you OK?" My knee gives a violent twitch. "Those are pretty serious shaving mishaps."

She shakes her head, a quick shiver. "Cat scratch."

"I thought your dad wouldn't let you have pets? Allergies, or whatever?" I know this small tidbit only because I caught her in a pet-impassioned trance last year at the pet store in the mall.

"No, there's this tomcat in our neighborhood. I was trying to play with him and he went all bonkers." She won't meet my eyes, and I let it go for now, because I don't want to make my only friend mad.

But the scratches don't look like they came from a cat.

"All right, children, children. Young-adult children. Give me your attention, please—this new schedule is driving me crazy, because as you know we only have forty-five minutes to commence learning everything we can learn about poetry, which you honestly couldn't learn everything about in forty-five years, or even four-hundred-and-fifty years, and I couldn't even pretend to understand the workings of our superintendent's mind when he cut us so short of time, and . . ."

 14

This is Mrs. Carstead, who near as I can tell is wound up like a clock spring all the time, or at least all of the time she's talking about English or education or anything relating to school, which is the only situation in which I've seen her. She is short, with hair in a long brown braid she twists into a circle at the base of her skull like half of the Princess Leia hairdo.

This giant cinnamon roll on her neck probably could tip her over if she thought more about it, because the woman can't weigh more than like a hundred pounds. She doesn't wear makeup and favors overalls and tennis shoes, which I hear is a continual fight with the principal.

I like her, though. She smiles a lot.

". . . I've probably used half of our forty-five minutes on this anti-superintendent rant, haven't I? Well, no matter. Let's use the rest of our time pondering the mind-set of William Carlos Williams. . . ." And she's off.

I tune her out for now and keep looking over at Cora, whose straight-ahead stare looks like it's chiseled in stone. I take out a piece of paper to write a note, but I have no idea what to say. For someone who loves words so much, why can't I find the right ones? I don't think those cuts are cat scratches.

I usually like writing better than I like talking, because I can look at the words before anybody sees them, and then change them if they look stupid. It's harder to do that when you are saying the words out loud, even though I rehearse them in my head as much as possible before they come out. Wow, that sounds crazy in itself. Obsessive compulsive? To say the least. I need to be able to check, double-check, just practice a little so I can be sure it works. I can't help it. No, no, no.

I write "Cora, are you OK?" but I already asked that.

Cora, I don't think those are cat scratches. I'm worried you are cutting yourself and I want to know why.

No, that's none of my business.

Cora, you're my friend and you have to tell me what is going on because I don't want you to hurt yourself. I think it's really stupid to want to hurt yourself.

No, she'll never speak to me again if I say that.

Cora, I wish I knew what was going on to make you sad.

Cora, stop it!

Finally I just write "I'm worried about you." And slip the note to her.

She unfolds it, glances at it, writes something, and pushes it back to me.

"No worries," it says. "I'm hunky dory, peachy keen."

I stare at her.

She looks at me, shrugs, and shakes her head.

ʘʘʘ

So "The Red Wheelbarrow" shrinks in importance in my mind after that. If it ever had any to begin with. At the sound of the bell, Cora and I walk out together without really saying anything, because everything I was rehearsing in my head sounded ridiculous, and she just isn't talking. She jumps on the bus with a wave, and I watch the doors whoosh shut.

Cora, stop it.

3. AnGst

angst /äNG(k)st/ n. a feeling of deep anxiety or dread; typically an unfocused one about the human condition or the state of the world in general.

☙❧

The walk home is a kaleidoscope of rehearsed phrases in every color and intonation. I want to call Cora tonight with the most compassionate, caring, and persuasive things to say that I ever could devise—whatever would help her stop hurting herself. If that's what she's doing. Why would she do that? See, this is just another example of how my troll powers do nobody any good. Words, written, spoken, or otherwise, are failing me, no matter what I can sense about your health. Ppppptttthhhh.

I trudge up the walk leading to my front door. The sight of our house usually makes me ultra happy, because it is new and beautiful and has room for Uncle Pasta. Flowers crawl up the sides of the walk, and there's an herb garden under the front window. Well-tended flowers and herbs, cared for by my father, Michael. This only seems weird if you know him, and might question whether this loving, gentle habit exists in contradiction with his pretty intense black-and-white view of the world. Today worry dulls the colors.

My mom is sitting on the porch drinking tea with our cat, Echo, on her lap. She is a writer of mystery novels, which is why I didn't see her at breakfast and why she's at home in the early afternoon. She gets up at five every morning and locks herself in a special writing room on the top floor of our house, sometimes for four hours, sometimes for eight or twelve, depending on her mood. She writes "cozies," which are mystery novels that read like buddy flicks: low body count, not too much blood, but lots of funny banter between the main characters, who in her latest series are English teachers who quote Shakespeare to fit any given situation.

Her name is Isabelle, and she looks like an Isabelle, which is small with long dark hair and dark eyes. Dangerous eyes, my dad calls them, which I think is a reference to sex but could be because she cusses like a Hell's Angel.

This is another verification of my troll status: she's beautiful and forward and strong—not a hive nor a hesitation to be found. I am utterly sure she never rehearses anything she says, which gets her in trouble sometimes, but she cares not at all. Oh, and did I mention her favorite novel of all time is *To Kill a Mockingbird?* Hence my name.

"Harper, honey. How was school today? Tell me something you learned."

This is her standard, annoying daily question. My regular angst is just so uninteresting, I can't imagine, even though I'm maybe her daughter, that it would be any fun to listen to. "I learned how to appropriately utilize my space. It was fascinating," I shrug. "Whose butt did Eloise kick today?" Eloise is the youngest of her English teacher heroines.

"Eloise actually engaged in a little kissy-face with her love interest today. I got bored with it, so I only wrote for two hours, then I came downstairs to watch Buffy." She's referring to the old TV series *Buffy the Vampire Slayer*, and she has every episode, every season, on Blu-ray. Don't ask.

"Hm," I say, shaking my head. "And whom did Buffy destroy today?" I can always get her off on a tangent about Buffy or Eloise, so sometimes she forgets the nosy questions.

Mom puts the cat down to adjust the waist of her blue shorts, shorts that look suspiciously like Dad's boxers. I would like to go to work every day in my husband's underwear, that's for sure.

"Oh, just a bunch of monsters. You're changing the subject. How's Cora?"

My mom loves Cora because they're both extreme smart alecks. I debate for like one second whether to tell her about what I think Cora is doing with the cutting, but I don't. I'm afraid Mom will want to call Cora's dad and then Cora'll truly never speak to me again.

"She's OK. You should've heard her verbally lay out this guy Mike when he tried a cheesy pickup line on her. It was glorious to behold."

My mom cocks her head at me, appraising. Her hair is in a braid that falls over the left shoulder of her Guns N' Roses T-shirt, and she looks like a girl even though she's forty-five. "Now, really, back to the subject. How's Harper? How's my beeyouteeful, smart little girl? How's Algebra 3/4?"

I snort. "Algebra is a bad, bad place for beeyouteeful smart little girls. It's like the ninth circle of hell for us BSLGs, don'tcha know? Today Mr. Thompson wrote a question on the board about those infamous X's and Y's, and he asked me to give the answer out loud, right then, in front of the entire class. Now, I'm sure it was an extremely simple question, being as how it's only the second week of school and the second year of algebra, but all I could do was stare at it like an idiot."

"So what happened? Did you eventually try to answer?"

"He said, 'Harper, can I ask you another question? If I told you to stand on your head, would you do it?'"

I see a wicked gleam in her eye. "And you said . . . ?"

"I said, 'If I thought it'd help me get an *A*.' He didn't like it. He harrumphed and swished his knuckles at me like he was washing his hands of me—and then he called on someone else. Some of the kids laughed though."

Mom sighs. "I was always terrible at numbers. Great at spelling words like 'theorem' and 'formula,' though. Even 'Pythagorean' couldn't throw me." She strokes Echo, who still purrs on her lap. "Hey, what'd you do to Peter? He moped his way right out the door today."

Now it's my turn to sigh. "I told him he was getting sick. He has a date tonight."

"Oh, right. The fabulous Charles. I'm sure Pete'll be stunning even wrapped in a stuffy nose."

Suddenly the glass of tea she's holding slips from her hand. In a slow-motion symphony, I see the tea hurdling the edge of the glass and splashing her hand as she jerks to recover it. I can see Echo the black puma cat leaping off her lap as elbows flail, hear the screaming protest of the glass as it explodes onto the patio concrete, and vaguely register the list of four-letter words that accompany and follow the crash.

"Son of a *bitch*!" is the end note as she stands to wipe tea from her lap. "How the hell did that happen?"

I bend and start picking up shards from around her bare feet. "You dropped the tea, Mom. No big deal. Don't move, or you'll cut yourself."

Echo has jumped clear of the broken glass and sits in front of the door, licking tea from his fur.

21

Mom sits back down and shakes her hands while I pick up glass. "Why am I so goofy these days?" she groans. "First, I tripped over Echo and ended up ass over teakettle on the front lawn, remember? Then, the other week—you were gone on your first day of school—I was cleaning up the breakfast dishes and I dropped that serving plate right into the dishwasher. Blammo! I know I'm a Sagittarius and thus predisposed to klutziness, but this is ridiculous."

"I'm sure it's just a glitch. You can't expect perfection all the time." I set the shards on the table.

"Yes, yes I can," she growls. "From myself I can. And Buffy."

"Well, she's not perfect either." I pat her shoulder and start for the door, scooping Echo up. "Last I checked, a superhero who kills vampires isn't supposed to be in love with one."

"*Touché.* Dinner's at six."

4. DaYdReaM

daydream /ˈdā drēm/ n. a series of pleasant thoughts that direct one's attention from the present.

⊙⊙⊙

I head up to my room on the pretext that I am going to do homework, but really it's Friday, and I'm going to sit in my room with the idea, the fantasy wonderland in which I reside, that I'm getting ready for a date with Larson McCready. Then I'm going to figure out what to say to Cora.

The desk in my room is a combination of form and function, with a computer and a thesaurus/dictionary on one side and a lighted mirror and a box of makeup on the other. I keep the mirror light on the lowest possible setting because you can't see pores very well that way. I take an "ignorance is bliss" standpoint on pore size.

So, Harper. I say to myself as I peer-carefully-into the dimly lit mirror. *What are you going to wear on your date with Larson tonight? And where are you going?*

I'm going to wear a stunning pair of very expensive jeans that hug my curves like a two-year-old with separation anxiety, a pair of ridiculously high stiletto heels that make my legs look as long as prehistoric redwoods, and a designer blouse that makes my boobs look both large and perky.

And we're going to dinner at Mikaelos, chuckles self, *which as you know is the most expensive and romantic restaurant in Pinewood.*

Self continues: *This makeup I am applying now makes zits disappear instantaneously and gives me hair that cascades. It's a magical makeup utilized by all the top models, which is why they look so perfect. I'm told it makes cellulite go away as well.*

Well, I say to myself. *It sounds like you are going to have a wonderful time. Are you going to go all the way with Larson?*

Oh, no! confirms self. *Larson is a gentleman. He wouldn't try to get into my pants until long after we have professed our profound love for one another.*

I look into the mirror with the strategic lighting. *You go for it, self. Larson is never going to know what hit him.*

෨෨෨

"Cora? It's me."

"Hey, chickadee. Howzit going?"

"I'm fine. How are you doing?" Ask her. Ask her now.

"I'm peachy. So, do you want to watch a movie tonight? I'd love to get out of this house—my uncle is here visiting my dad and they turn into beer-swilling knuckleheads when they're together. He hasn't been around since I was like twelve and I don't remember my dad being this much of an idiot back then. Anyway, I'd prefer to come over there if you wanna scope some flicks."

She sounds almost normal. I'm still worried. "OK, sure. Let's 'scope.' I think my mom is cooking dinner, though, so give us a couple of hours and then come on over."

"Your mom is cooking dinner?" There's a short pause.

"Sorry, I was cleaning out my ears. Come again? Your MOM is cooking dinner?"

"Oh, stop it. She told me Dad came home from work all huffy today. I guess his boss stampeded all over an idea he had for a shaving cream commercial, and then commandeered an idea he had for an Old Spice commercial. He said he felt emasculated and someone else had to cook."

"That sucks," says Cora. "He should start his own agency. Or open his own restaurant. Don't you think his mood is gonna crack even more when he has to eat Isabelle's cooking?" she laughs, a shrill cackle that she cuts off midsquawk. I decide right then to spend dinner rehearsing what to say to her when she comes to watch the movie.

"We keep telling him that. His ideas are so good, as evidenced by the fact that his boss is stealing them. But I think he's scared. Starting your own business is hard—I guess like eighty-five percent of them fail in their first year."

I hear some raucous male laughter through the phone. "Gotta go," Cora says hurriedly. "I'll see you in a couple."

Click.

I stare at the phone. The numbers seem to gather in the middle, then expand into a circle like an old-fashioned rotary phone. Maybe that's because I need an old phone, E.T.-style, to phone home to my troll family. Maybe they, in their infinite and ugly wisdom, can tell me what to say to Cora, and to Larson, and to everyone else I ever meet, so they will be entranced, illuminated, informed, and influenced by Yours Truly.

5. TRiCKeRY

trickery /ˈtrik(ə)rē/ n. the practice of deception.

⊙⊙⊙

The household had increased in number since I went upstairs after school. My mom's in the kitchen, judging by the unidentifiable smells. Uncle Pasta and my dad sit in the living room watching the Food Network, which is the main thing my dad will watch besides ESPN, and which is the only thing Dad watches that Uncle Pasta likes.

My uncle favors the BBC and musicals and anything filmed before 1950, which Dad insists he likes just fine, but which I know he hates, because every time there's something on that's black and white or has characters who spontaneously burst into song, he fidgets. He's really tall, my dad, and when something like *Singin' in the Rain* is on the television, he tries to scrunch down into this little ball on the couch, and he spends the entire time with fingers tap-tap-tapping on his knees.

I run in and throw myself on the couch between them. "Hello handsomes! How were your days? Old Spice is a terrible cologne, Dad. You're better off. And Uncle Peter, are you excited about your date? Charles must be salivating in anticipation."

"Harper!" my dad chuffs. "Don't be crude." He shoots me a disapproving look and runs a hand through his closely cropped blond hair. I'm not sure how Dad feels about Uncle Peter's sexual orientation. Uncomfortable, I think.

I cross my legs, the very picture of demure obedience. "Sorry, Daddy. I'm sure Charles is looking forward to your date as much as you are, Uncle Peter."

Uncle Peter nods from his position next to me, and I can see the smile twitching at his lips. "I don't hear you sneezing, *mi amore*. Does that mean I'm not going to get sick after all? My nose hasn't stuffed up all day."

"Hey, yeah! I haven't sneezed since I came downstairs. Maybe you dodged a bullet with the orange juice." I squeeze his shoulder.

My dad slaps his hands on his knees and bolts up from the couch, pulling his tie from around his neck and tossing it on the floor. "Oh, for God's sake, you two. You and your crazy troll nonsense. Harper, you can*not* sense when other people get sick just because you sneeze around them or your nose twitches or any other hogwash. Jesus Christ!" He stomps around the couch and through the door to the backyard, slamming it behind him.

Holy cow. He sure is puffed up. Ouch. I didn't mean to make his day worse with my stupid useless senses.

Uncle Pasta puts an arm around my shoulders. "He's just upset about work, honey. He knows you have this ability. Remember when he got the chicken pox? You knew a week before the first little pock even showed up."

"Who cares? I told you—it's not an ability, or a gift, or anything." The fingers sitting on my lap look like shaky octopus tentacles. I squeeze them into fists. "It doesn't do anybody any good to know they're getting sick. You might as well tell them they're going to—oh, I don't know—you might as well tell them the sky is falling. They wouldn't be able to prevent it—just sit in fear and horror until it happened. At least without me around they could go about their business in ignorant bliss."

Frustrated, I shut up and return to my thoughts to rehearse some more conversations with Cora. Maybe Uncle Peter can help keep Mom from crucifying dinner, because what he's saying to me ain't working. I still feel like a joke.

ⓞⓞⓞ

"Mmmmm." Uncle Pasta smacks his lips. "Delectable, little sis. You're practically the reincarnation of Martha Stewart."

Mom says, "Martha Stewart's not dead. How about Betty Crocker?"

"Mom, I don't think Betty Crocker is even a real person—just a brand name."

My dad has been sitting at the head of the table since Mom brought a serving plate filled with her mystery dish and placed it with a flourish in the center. He's tapping his knife on the table and tracing the navy-blue line that decorates our dinner plates with his thumb.

"Why don't you look that up, Harper?" he says. "Maybe Izzy's the reincarnation of Duncan Hines." He oozes sarcasm, and I don't know how to respond.

However, my mother does. "Michael Southwood. What is your problem? We all know that you are the only one here who can cook. You're the only one here who can look at a product and come up with the perfect spin from which to sell it. You're the only one who understands the difference between a carburetor and a chassis."

She stabs a large knife into the middle of her dish and starts sawing. "You're the only one here who can do lots of different things, but one thing you apparently *cannot* do is have a sense of perspective about one bad day amongst millions of good ones that are chock full of blessings and love and support. For the love of Peter, Paul, and Mary, re*lax* and enjoy this dish I invented just for you. It's called Delicious Advertisement."

Dad had stopped tapping as soon as he heard Mom's raised voice, and now his thumb halts its circular journey as well. They stare at each other, him defiant and her annoyed. Uncle Pasta looks at me, eyebrows lifted all the way to his kinky hairline. I've always thought the expression "you could cut the tension with a knife" to be a ridiculous cliché, but I guess sometimes people say these types of things ad nauseam because they're true.

After what seems like ten minutes, but is probably only ten seconds, Dad drops the knife. He runs his hands through his hair, closes his eyes, and sighs. "You're right. Harper, I'm sorry. I just felt tremendous about that shaving cream layout, and Bill stomped all over it. And then the Old Spice jingle was fantastic, if I do say so myself, and he snatched it out from under me. Said it dovetailed nicely with an idea he'd already been working on, which is bull. Bill hasn't done anything for days but sit in his office texting his mistress."

Uncle Peter sucks in his breath and shows a wide-eyed, ooh-gossip face. "Your boss texts his mistress at work? How do you know that?"

Dad scoops some food from the platter to his plate and stabs it with his fork. "He got drunk at a conference in Chicago and told me all about it. He's an idiot." He grabs a huge forkful of food and shovels it down. He chews. He pauses and seems to rework it inside his mouth. He chews again. He swallows. "Hmm. What did you say was in this, honey?"

Mom says brightly, "I didn't. It's biscuits, with pasta over the top and pieces of chicken and beans and corn. Then I tried to make this wine sauce with all sorts of those herbs and spices thrown in—you know that spice rack you have above the oven?" She gestures behind her head, toward the kitchen. "Of course you do. Well, you're always randomly grabbing and pouring those things in all willy-nilly, and I thought I should do the same thing and get this fabulously exciting and surprising taste, like you do. Do you like it?"

"Sure, honey, it's delicious." He looks down at the plate, and seems to have an internal debate about whether to go in again. He does, and when he closes his eyes this time, I think it's so he can concentrate hard enough to make the food go down.

Mom scoops some of . . . of whatever it is . . . onto my plate. "Try it, honey."

I take a big bite, even though I'm scared, just to make her feel better. I can taste all of the terrific spices Dad uses when he cooks, sure, but when they are ALL together in a single dish they are . . . not so good. Really bad, in fact. I close my eyes, just like Dad, to get it down.

When I open them up, Mom's looking at me. She gives me a huge wink, and right then I know what she's done.

"It's delicious, Mom."

I glance at Dad and open my eyes wide in an Oscar-winning expression which begs, *Please, Daddy, don't ever let her cook again.*

He smothers a grin that says, *Of course, honey. Never again.*

Miss Bakener, eat your heart out. I say, "Thanks for cooking for us tonight."

6. Ceaseless

ceaseless /'sēs ləs/ adj. constant and unending.

⊙⊙⊙

I'm on the big poofy couch in our living room, aimlessly clicking through pay-per-view movies when the doorbell rings. I hop over to open the door.

"Hey, Chiquita banana," says Cora, pushing her way past me. "What'd you find? Anything good? And please don't say you want to watch *The Shawshank Redemption* again. There is absolutely nobody hot in that movie, and there are almost no funny parts." Before I can say anything, she heads up the stairs to my room. "Let's watch up in your room, OK? OK."

I trudge up the stairs behind her. *Cora, I'm really worried about you. I read about self-mutilation today and it said something about people choosing pain over emptiness. Are you feeling empty, Cora? And why is that? Do you miss your mom? Of course you do.* Stupid, stupid. It all sounded stupid. I sound like a big pathetic dork and my knee is twitching so badly I can hardly make it up the stairs.

When I get to the door of my room to look in, Cora is

34

standing by the side wall, on which I'd hung posters of Albert Einstein and William Shakespeare and a lighthouse. I have a thing about lighthouses even though I live in the mountains. There's also this really cool poster-sized photo of a little rowboat sitting on a beach in Thailand, with a clear blue ocean behind it that stretches out forever and drops over the edges of the print like the world is flat. So, I favor lighthouses and boats because they are both protective structures.

But I don't know how to protect Cora.

"I don't like the boat one, did I tell you that already?" she says. "When I look at that huge body of water behind it, and imagine myself rowing out in that rickety little boat, and then when I get over to this part," she traces her finger over to the edge of the poster. "I just fall off. Forever." She looks at me, and her green almond eyes are heavy lidded and tired. "I don't like that."

Before I can respond, she shakes herself, grabs me and hauls me over to the bed. She's wearing pajama bottoms with little frogs on them and a green T-shirt. She hops up on the bed with me in tow and starts jumping up and down. "Pillow fight! Pillow fight!" Then she collapses. "Just kidding. Let's find a movie. I prefer one with Orlando Bloom, only not one of those hobbit ones. How about one of the *Pirates of the Caribbean* movies?"

"Sure, we've only seen those about fifty times."

Cora crosses her legs and grabs a brush to sit behind me on the bed while I start the movie. "Can I brush your hair? Good." She undoes my ponytail and starts to brush it out.

Ow.

"Sorry. You have really pretty hair, Harper. Did you know that?"

I pull one piece around and follow its zigzag path with my finger. "Sure, if you're into big bushy shrubs, like the ones in my front yard. My front yard is pretty, I guess. If you're a gardener.

But I don't think Larson is a gardener. He's a basketball player."

Cora tugs my hair tight and starts to braid it. "Oh, bah. Screw Larson and all his testosterone-y friends. They don't know anything." She finishes the braid and lays it over my shoulder like my mom wears it. "See, you look just like Isabelle."

"Sure I do. And my front yard looks like the Garden of Eden." Since she's sitting cross-legged, I can see the scratches on her right leg. *Now is the time.* I touch the scratches, and she recoils, pushing my hand away. "Cora. These aren't really cat scratches, are they? Please tell me."

She jumps up and moves back to the boat picture, flattening her palm against it. "Sure, I told you. Nasty ol' neighborhood tomcat." She slaps her hand on the front of the boat, right where it's going over the edge. "Mean little sucker."

"Cora, please." Think, think. "I want to . . . I want to help. To listen."

"That Captain Jack Sparrow, he's crazy," she says. "I can't believe he's such a—such a—"

"Are they really from a cat, Cora? Really?"

I don't think she's going to say anything. Then she crunches up her shoulders and comes to sit with me on the edge of the bed. "No, I did them to myself." She pulls her knee up and traces the cuts with a finger.

"But *why*? Why would you hurt yourself?" *I don't understand. This is so awful.* My funny, beautiful friend.

Cora reaches behind her back for one of my decorative purple pillows, and sets it under her knees. A royal pillow for the princess in pain.

"You know the funny thing?" she muses. "It didn't hurt —not really. I just took the razor and gave it a little *whoosh* down one side and then completed the cross, or the plus sign, or whatever it looks like to you, and as soon as the blood came up it was like I could breathe again. It was like relief. It was like the pain and the blood meant I was really alive."

I jump up. "It was like you were really alive because you were BLEEDING? The pain made you relieved?" I feel like I've just materialized on another planet. A bad one. "You could breathe again because you're permanently scarring yourself? Cora, are you crazy? I can't believe you would do something ludicrous like that. I thought you were smarter than that." I pace back and forth in front of her. My arms flail like they are their own living creatures, and I can't stop the words that gush out of my mouth like vomit. It's like I'm barfing all over my best friend, screaming against the stupidity of hurting yourself on purpose.

Everything I'd rehearsed, the most supportive, compassionate, and influential things I was going to say fly out the window and land in the front yard shrubbery. Harper, the ill-tempered, malformed troll, is here full force, and I watch Cora draw up both knees and wrap her arms around them like she could disappear into a little ball. Still I can't stop.

She hangs her head on her knees, turns her beautiful green eyes toward me and stares, mute. Any lights that had been on in the emerald irises fade and dim as I rave, and the colors turn muddy. Her lip quivers only once, when I start to cry and can't stop shaking my head.

When I finally wind down and start apologizing, profusely apologizing, saying "I don't know what came over me" and "I was just so worried about you," she just stays in that little ball, looking at me. She won't say any more, and she stays quiet and compressed through the whole movie.

When she gets up to leave I hug her as hard as I can and tell her again how sorry I am. Still she looks like she wants to disappear into that ball, even when she stands up straight and walks out the door.

Cora, stop it.

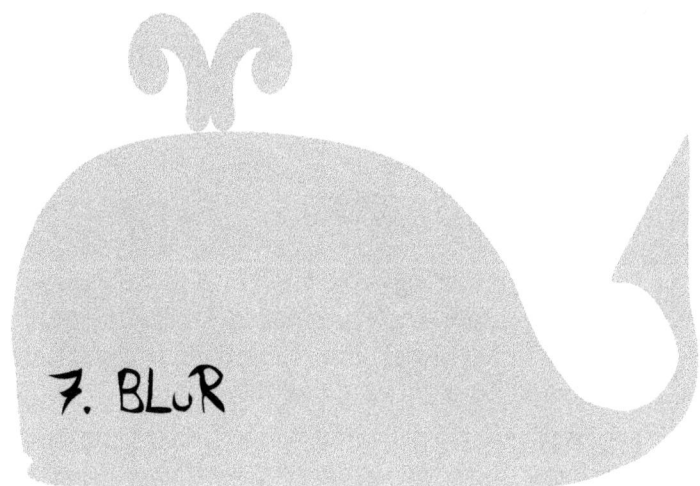

7. BLUR

blur /blər/ v. make or become less clear or distinct.

ⓥⓥⓥ

"Hello?"

"Hi, Mr. Perkins. May I please speak to Cora?"

"She's not here, Harper. She said she was going for a walk, like physical fitness's her number one priority. You two get into it last night? She's been in a shit-rotten mood all day."

God, I hate myself. "Yes, and it's all my fault. Will you please, please tell her I called?"

"Sure. You two need to work this out. I don't like dealing with her when she's like this. There are no females here to handle the massive PMS, ya know? Take care of it."

Click.

Was this or was this not the second time in two days I'd gotten dead air on the Perkins's line? If I had that man as a father, maybe I'd cut myself, too. No, that's not true. I think if I had him as a father, I would bide my time until I could emancipate myself and then I would just go as far away as possible. Maybe

I'd join the Peace Corps. Or the French Foreign Legion. What do you do in the French Foreign Legion, anyway? I should look it up.

No, I am one lucky little troll.

ⓞⓞⓞ

The whole family's sitting at the breakfast table, eating something I'm sure my dad cooked, because it smells really good.

"Harper! Come and have some *ebel-skeebers*," says Uncle Pasta. "They are amazing."

I see a pile of round pastries covered in whipped cream, powdered sugar, and some raspberries. "What in the world are *ebel-skeebers*?" I sit down for a huge bite. They're wonderful, like a sweet pancake puffed up in a ball. "Wow, these are fantastic. Do you spell that with an *e*?"

Dad grins. "I don't know how you spell it, Harper. I just know how to make it. The looking-up is your jurisdiction."

He's in a much better mood today. I'm glad *someone* is. "Uncle Peter, how was your date with Charles?"

"It was lovely, just like you thought it would be. He'th a thweetie." He bats his eyelids at my father, who just smiles and shakes his head. Wow, he *is* in a good mood. "What movie did you girls watch last night? I thought I heard the divine Orlando Bloom calling to me through the keyhole?"

"You did, and he is. Divine, I mean. Although I'm more partial to Johnny Depp, myself. Heavy eyeliner and all, he is brilliant." *Not that I even saw him. Cora, where are you? I'm so, so sorry.*

Mom hasn't said anything since I came down. She pokes her fork in and out of the berries without actually spearing any up to her mouth. "Mom, are you OK? You don't like the *ebel-skeebers*?"

Dad reaches out and pats her arm. "Izzy, what's the matter? Aren't you feeling well? *Ebel-skeebers* will fix what's ailin' ya, I promise."

She stares down at her plate, rolling the berries back and forth along the underside of the fork tines. "The *ebelwatchahooies* taste great." She looks up now, and her eyes are huge. "The problem is, I'm not *seeing* them so well."

Dad and I look at each other. *What?*

Uncle Pasta swerves his chair around so his knees brush up against the side of her chair, and he spreads her eyelids apart. "Do you think you have some dust stuck in them? Here, let me look." This he says after he's got her pinned like a butterfly on a board.

Pushing his hands out of the way, Mom says, "Don't. There's nothing in them. They just don't seem to be working right —things are sort of blurry, and then some things I see double."

Dad says, "Do you have a headache? I've heard that migraines can cause some pretty severe vision problems." He gets up and stands behind her, rubbing her shoulders.

She rubs her temples. "No, not really. My head feels OK. My eyes are the things that pain me, in a figurative sense. It's very weird, and I don't like it—I'm disturbed."

"Well, we knew *that* already. That's nothing new." I smile, trying to make a joke of it. *See, it's OK? There's nothing wrong.* "See? I haven't sneezed all morning, and my nose doesn't itch a bit."

OK, so the joke was stupid and ill timed. That's what I get when I am sans rehearsal. But it's true, I'm not exhibiting any signs of troll power. It seems to make her feel better.

"You're right. It's probably nothing." She scoops up some berries and pops them in.

"But you're going to the doctor today anyway, right?" my father lectures. "I don't think vision problems are anything you should try and pass off as 'no big deal.' These are your precious eyes, honey." His lips purse with concern and he watches the top of her head as he rubs, as if he can see through her skull and down into her optic nerve.

She gives him a salute. "OK, Daddy." He does this paternal thing with everybody sometimes, and while I find it condescending, she just blows him off. I guess in twenty years of knowing someone, you have to learn to blow some things off.

I wonder if Larson would do things I felt like blowing off? I can't imagine wanting to do that with him. I don't think he would be condescending or jerky with his soul mate, I'm sure. Sure.

We sit silently for the rest of breakfast, and when I leave for school I hug her extra-hard, even though I'm sure it's nothing.

ⓞⓞⓞ

Cora wouldn't return my calls all weekend, so this morning's walk to school is chock full of trepidation and angst. I ward off hives at every turn, and I feel like the list of worries crawling down my throat is sure to be projectile vomited any second now. My best (read: *only*) friend is furious with me, my mom's feeling sick although my body gives me no clues about this, we're supposed to start appropriately using our voices today in Acting, and this weekend of stupid comments on my part has taught me that muteness is better than using my voice, appropriately or not. Who knows what torture will be rendered on the physically unfit in PE? And to top it all off—a moldy cherry on a melted, sugar-free ice cream sundae—today is the day we start dissecting cats.

ⓞⓞⓞ

You know, there is an interesting urban legend at Pinewood High School regarding cat dissection. Sometime way back in the eighties, there was a student named Mari Wulkerstein, AKA Scary Mari. She was the original Goth queen of Pinewood, back when Goths were called Punks. She apparently threw a fit about the inhumanity of cat dissection, even though I'm pretty sure we aren't murdering the cats (they're dead when we get them). So she snuck into the school the night before cat dissection, kidnapped the cats, and took them away to give them a proper burial.

If one believes the entire legend, she was led away from the pet cemetery in chains, wailing and cursing the injustice of a system that allows cat desecration. I'm pretty sure what actually happened to Mari was detention in the form of Saturday school and the forced return of cat carcasses back to the Anatomy lab. Much less interesting.

I wish I had the nerve to take such a public and passionate stand for something I cared about. Scary Mari is like cool scary.

The courtyard buzzes like a frenetic beehive, with kids sprawled on concrete benches, hysterically finishing the homework they'd avoided all weekend. Cora sits on one of the benches, hands at her sides, backpack unopened. She's looking up at one of the giant trees growing inside each of the concrete squares the kids are sitting on. On which the kids are sitting. Whatever.

Cora, please talk to me. I'm so, so sorry.

I'm extremely hivey and nervous, but I walk toward her anyway. When I get close, she looks at me. Her face is unreadable.

"Why does a flamingo pull up one leg?" she says.

A joke. Oh, thank goodness, it's a joke. "I don't know. Why does a flamingo pull up one leg?"

"Well, if he pulled them both up, he'd fall over!"

I throw my arms around her. "Cora, I'm so sorry. I just . . ."

"I know what you just. Let's forget about it, OK? You're right, the cutting is stupid and I shouldn't do it. Can we pretend it never happened and start over?"

"Let's do that." I'm just so relieved that we're OK, I completely ignore a niggling little voice that says, *She didn't say she wouldn't do it, now did she? She also still hasn't told me why she's doing it in the first place.*

We're friends again, and I'll have to worry about the other stuff later. Pesky little voices about cutting and Mom's vision problems pale right now in comparison with having my only real friend back.

On happy reflection, the rest of the day turned out so much better. I flew through Acting on wings of relief. I didn't even care when Miss Bakener wanted me to talk in Gibberish to Cade Castell.

We had to pick everyday activities and make our partner perform them without any real words, just by asking through facial expression and vocal tone. I was supposed to get him to untie his shoes without saying, "Cade, untie your shoes" in any actual language or recognizable gesture, like pointing to his shoelaces.

We stood there, eye to eye. Then I crossed my arms, looked down at the floor, and said, "*Uhnh.*"

Cade untied his shoes.

Miss Bakener said we must have talked about what I was going to say beforehand.

Yes, of course. We cheated at Gibberish.

8. DiSSeCTioN

dissection /dī sekSHən/ n. the action of dissecting a body or plant to study its internal parts; a very detailed analysis of a text or idea.

☙❦❧

Anatomy, however, promises to be another story. My wings droop like Icarus under the scorching sun when I enter the room. My nostrils are immediately assaulted with the smell of formaldehyde, and my heart breaks like Scary Mari when I see the lumps, covered in sheets, sitting atop the lab tables that line the perimeter of the room.

Cat dissection. There oughta be a law.

"OK, kiddos. Hurry up and come on in. We have a lot of introductory stuff to do before we can take off these sheets." Mr. Wolfram waves us in, obviously much more excited about scalpels and cat guts than the rest of us, who all sort of skulk into the room.

I have to hand it to Mr. Wolfram, though. With his signature Hawaiian shirts and cargo pants, paired with constant

boundless enthusiasm, he makes the lab feel like kitty-cat Mardi Gras. Science and school make him so happy I'm even willing to forgive him calling us kiddos. The jury's still out on cat dissection, though. The smell, at least, is unforgivable.

"Have a seat, have a seat," says Mr. Wolfram. "The first thing you need to do is introduce yourself to your partner, if you haven't already met. On your desk is a list of the class, divided into pairs. Find your name on the list, find your partner, and go sit with him or her behind one of the cat bags."

Oh, God. I didn't know this torture came in pairs. Panicked, I search the list for my name. Please, give me Allison, the heavy girl from gym class. Give me the quiet girl in the corner; give me Dennis Porter, whom I've known since birth and who still picks his nose, but that's OK. Give me—Oh. My. God.

"So I guess we're like, partners." And there he stands, Larson McCready. In all his glory.

And here come the hives. *Oh God, oh God, what do I say now? I haven't rehearsed anything, I didn't know this was going to happen, he is so beautiful and how come his eyelashes are so long and dark even though he's got blond hair and—Oh. My. God.* "Yes, it looks like we are." Brilliant.

"So, I guess we should go over and, like, pick us a kitty." He turns tail—no pun intended—and lopes toward one of the lab tables.

OK, Harper. Don't blow it now. Now is your chance to say something mind blowing. Awe inspiring. Something that will stop him in his tracks and send him home from school today with Harper on the brain. Something that will force him to drop to one knee and propose on the spot. Something . . . "Do they still have fur? I don't know if I can handle it if they have fur." Brilliant.

"Nah, don't worry. I think they're maybe already skinned. No fur." He slaps the bag. "Let's name ours Spike."

He's so handsome in his low-slung blue jeans. His hair kind of curls around the nape of his neck and he has three of the most precious freckles on the bridge of his nose. Do you think virile and studmuffiny-type boys would like having any part of their person referred to as "precious"? I think probably not.

"OK, kiddos. The first thing you need to do is take off the sheet covering your cat. It is being held in a protective plastic bag, and I'm afraid this kitty has seen the end of its protection. So I want you to put on your goggles and gloves, poke a hole in the plastic bag and drain the formaldehyde into the sink."

He shakes his now-gloved hands at us. "Formaldehyde is a known carcinogen. So limit your exposure, kiddos. Do not go around sniffing the stuff." At this point, Mr. Wolfram walks over to the electrical switches near the classroom door and flips on the new HVAC system. Powerful ventilation fans cyclone through the classroom. "Use your gloves now. Do NOT let the chemicals come into contact with your bare skin."

Larson just looks at me and smiles. Wow. One of his front teeth is a little crooked, and whereas Larson with perfect teeth would be toothpaste-model boy, Larson with one little smile flaw is character-boy mischievous, maybe just a teensy bit bad. Character-boy Larson is ever so much more attractive.

"Here's your goggles," he says.

I put them on and try a toothpaste smile of my own.

"You look like a bug," he says.

OK, OK. At least he's looking at me. *Now start reeling him in with scintillating conversation.* "Um, do you want me to empty the bag?" Uhnh.

"Nah, I'll do that," he says gallantly. He turns the scissors over in his fingers and starts jabbing them into the plastic. "Hey, so your name is Harper?"

He knows my name! "So, uh, how do you know my name, Larson?" Larson. Lllllarson. I can hear Uncle Pasta rolling the name over his tongue when I bring him home for dinner on our fourth date.

46

Larson takes the grungy scissors out of the bag and drops the bag in the sink. Liquid gurgles and sloshes and stinks to high heaven. *Why didn't Mr. Wolfram tell us to don nose plugs along with goggles and gloves?*

"Because of the partners list, dude. You're my partner, on the list. Why, how did you know *my* name?"

Oh, right. The list. "Um, it was of course from the list. Um, dude." So I'm pretty sure Lancelot never called Guinevere "dude." "So, what do we do next?"

"Now I think we cut the kitty." He turns around and yells, "Hey, Mr. Wolfram. Can we cut him now?"

Mr. Wolfram walks our way. "Harper and Larson. I'm so glad to see your fascination with the feline anatomy. Yes, we can 'cut the kitty' now." He turns from our table and addresses the group. "Class, here's what I want you to do: the fascia and connective tissue have already been removed, so what you're looking at are the muscles. There will be lines where dark and light-pink or white areas meet; this represents the space between muscles. Use these lines as a guide for separating muscles." He waves his hands over the pink and white areas.

"To separate muscles, use your blunt probe, not the pointy one, to pry the muscle bundles apart along these demarcations. Just glide your probe under the connective tissue. Be sure to note each muscle's points of attachment—that's their origin and insertion, kiddos. Then use your scissors to snip at one end of each muscle to expose any underlying muscles. Label each muscle you dissect with the numbered pins in your kit, and I'll come by to quiz each of you."

We all stare, except for Larson who's itching to slice and snip, I can tell. "Go ahead, get started," says Wolfram.

I spend the rest of the period trying to say funny and provocative things to Larson without barfing all over him from the formaldehyde smell, also from the fact that we are cutting something up which is better suited for sitting in laps and purring in ears. The closest I get to doing something cool is when we reach something called the brachioradialis muscle, and I label it correctly. He looks impressed. I think. I know Mr. Wolfram is.

As we clean up and store "Spike" for tomorrow, I rack my own brain for something to say so Larson'll be left with Harper on his.

"Larson?"

"Yeah?"

"Good luck in the game tonight. I'll be rooting for you."

"Harper?"

"Yes, Larson?"

"Basketball season doesn't start until November." He shakes his head. "See you tomorrow." And then he laughs. "Thanks for the advanced notice on the 'good luck' wishes, I guess." And then he's gone.

Oh yes, Harper. He'll think about you more later. He's got you on the brain now, allrighty. Whoopee.

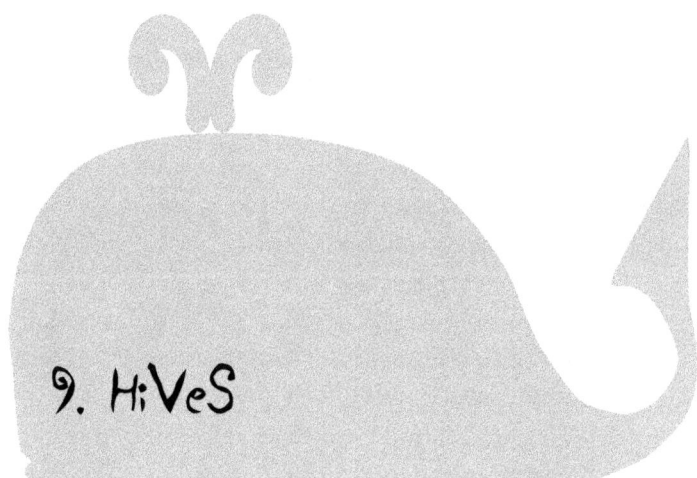

9. HiVeS

hives /hīvz/ n. a rash characterized by intensely itching welts.

⊚⊚⊚

I slide into my seat in Carstead's class and start fanning my chest. Basketball season doesn't start until November?! I should have just come right out and told him I'm a creature from another dimension and my kind doesn't know anything about sports. How could I be so stupid? I had the perfect opportunity to get his attention, and . . . well, I guess I did that. I got his attention, all right, and gave him a great story to tell his friends. "What? You got partnered with the guy who still picks his nose? That's nothing. Listen to THIS. . . ."

"Hey, chickadee." Cora appears suddenly, like a hailstorm. "What's wrong? You look like you just lost your favorite teddy bear. Hey, did I ever tell you about what happened with my favorite teddy bear? I lost it when I was five. It was tragic: I carried that thing everywhere, and when it was gone I cried for weeks. My mom bought me like five different new ones and none of them made any difference. I was devastated." Cora scooches her seat closer to throw an arm around my shoulders.

I shrug her off. "Does the teddy bear story have a point? Because a sad little bear disappearance that happened to you when you were five doesn't seem to compare with the complete and utter destruction of any potential love life I might have had once but now never will. It just doesn't!"

"Harper! What happened? You're freaking me out."

"Oh, it's Larson. He and I are partners for cat dissection."

Her eyes widen. "Partners! But that's awesome. . . . Doesn't that unit last for a whole week?"

"Two," I cry. "Oh, my God. How am I going to survive two weeks after what happened today?"

Cora's concerned face makes me want to cry. "Good grief, Harper. Did you propose? Did you rip off your shirt, grab your boobs and shout 'Here, take these, they're yours'? What happened?"

"No, no. I was simply trying to say something impressive. Something with pizzazz. Something that would make him remember me. But I got all twitterpated and couldn't think of anything, so I just blurted something out."

"OK, the suspense. I can't stand the suspense." She grabs my arms and shakes me. "*What did you say???*"

I can feel my shoulders and their involuntary slump. "I wished him good luck in his basketball game tonight. Told him I'd be rooting for him."

"You didn't."

"I did. I did!" That last one must've come out as a wail, because people are staring.

"Oh, honey. You know basketball season doesn't start until November?"

Her face is so sympathetic I want to smack her. My look could melt metal. "Well, yes, I know that *now*, thank you very not at all. I know it after he told me I looked like a bug and then laughed at my utter lack of sports comprehension. I'm never going to get over him—I really should be returning to my troll family as we speak. No, better yet—I should just search out a family of howler monkeys and join them—they'd love me for who I am: sports debilitated, zit ridden, and pathetic." My shoulders slump further, if that's possible.

Cora reaches over and hugs me. Her thin arms are strong, and I hug her back and try not to cry. My knees twitch, so violently I nearly lurch off the chair. I pull away to look at her. She's smiling, a real smile, and her green eyes are bright.

What is going on with my knee? She looks fine—almost relieved. And intent—she looks intent—like she's concentrating really hard on something.

"It's going to be OK, I promise. He doesn't even deserve you." She pats my knee, and it twitches again. "Hey, I have something for you."

"OK, children. Young-adult children. Today I am going to leave you alone." Mrs. Carstead waves a sheaf of papers. "I need some more time to grade your 'Red Wheelbarrow' analyses, so I want you to do an individual poetry project. I would like you to go through your textbook and find a poem that speaks to you, and then be ready tomorrow to tell me what it says and what it means to you. I'm sorry I don't have a more interactive lesson plan, but that's life in the fast lane. So do some work, 'K? We'll interact tomorrow."

With that, she pads across the floor, plops down and raises her feet up over her desk. She starts flipping through our essays, and I'm sure people are thinking, *Uh-oh, if the principal could see her now: no lesson plans and tennis shoes up on the desk, she'd be in truh-bull!* Actually, I'm sure no other high school student even thinks like that, or considers the teacher and her status with administration. Just me.

I look over at Cora, who isn't even paying attention: she's digging through her backpack.

52

"Hey," I say, trying to shake myself free of the Larson debacle. Maybe I could concentrate on poetry—not love poetry, mind you—and forget. "I think we should find an Emily Dickinson poem. Did you know you can sing every one of her gazillion poems to the tune of 'The Yellow Rose of Texas'? I tried it—it's true." I start humming, but she ignores me and keeps digging.

Finally, she pulls something free. "Here," she says. "I want you to have this."

She drops the thing in my hand. It's a bracelet: a silver braid, shiny and delicate, with a small diamond on either side of the clasp. "It's beautiful, Cora," I whisper. "Where did you get it? Why are you giving it to me now? Are you psychic and you predicted I was going to make a fool of myself today, so I'd of course need something to make me feel better?"

"It's platinum, and those are real diamonds." She wraps it around my wrist and connects the gems together to clasp it. She's looking at the floor when she says, "It was my mother's."

I gasp. *Why on God's green earth would she be giving me something that belonged to her mother, who died?* "Cora!" I yelp, then I remember we're supposed to be doing a poem analysis. I lower my voice. "I couldn't possibly take this. Why aren't you wearing it?"

"Because I want you to have it," she murmurs. "End of discussion."

"But Cora . . ." I wonder if she's doing this to get me to forget about the cutting? I can't forget. I won't be able to stop worrying unless she really stops.

"No buts," she shushes me. "You can wear it on your first date with Larson, who doesn't deserve you by the way, but you might as well go out with him, you know, just to give the poor guy a break." She pats the bracelet and pushes my hand back toward me.

I snort. This, also, causes people to stare, and now even

Mrs. Carstead gives me a look. "All right. If you insist, I'll go out with him." *I'll have to think more about possible reasons for this. But later, when I'm over the Larson major malfunction.* "And thank you—this is beautiful. I'll wear it always. Now come on, let's find our poem and get outta here."

We spend the rest of the period searching our books for poems that speak to us. Cora finds a limerick, which is pretty much a poem's version of a dumb joke. Perfect for her. I find one by Karl Shapiro called "The Fly" and it starts with this line: "Oh hideous little bat, the size of snot." Perfect.

After the bell, I walk with Cora to the bus loop. She stands on the bottom step of the bus and smiles and waves, until the driver barks at her to get in. Then she waves from the window until the bus pulls out and drives away.

My knee twitches until she's out of sight. I wonder about it all the way home.

10. FLuMMoXeD

flummoxed /'flǝmǝkst/ adj. bewildered or perplexed.

✺✺✺

The walk to and from school is intended for contemplation, right? But I don't know what to contemplate, what to obsess over, what to dismiss. I'm supposed to be winding down from the day, but every step twists up my spine like stripes on a barbershop pole. I start rewinding my entire day. . . .

First, I should have called my mom at lunch to see what the doctor said, but I was floating like a helium-filled balloon about making up with Cora. I look down at the bracelet on my wrist and think about my crazy knee. What was that all about? She seemed so happy when she left.

And then there's Larson. God, I still can't believe I was so stupid, that I'd opened my mouth and sludge came out. Maybe he'll give me a second look. Maybe he'll forget all about my little faux pas, and tomorrow I'll say something charming. Sure, and maybe all those little kitties in Anatomy will spring to life and scamper away. Free *A*'s for everyone, and no more humiliation for me.

My dad's and Uncle Peter's cars are in the driveway. Hmm . . . that's strange—it's only four. I walk in.

"Hey, what's going on? Is it everybody's day off?" My heart skips a beat.

My mom sits in the middle of the couch, with a man on either side. Dad is rubbing her lower back, and she and my uncle are leafing through a book. They all look very serious.

Oh, my God. What is happening?

"We're waiting for the right time to go back to the doctor and swig some more sugar syrup," says Mom. "I have to confirm my lack of diabetes."

"The doctor thinks you have diabetes? That could cause your vision problems?" Diabetes sounds bad, but not terminal. I don't think it's deadly. She could deal with it. I hope.

Uncle Pasta stands and cocks his hip, very effete all of a sudden. He does this queen stuff for my mom sometimes because it makes her laugh. "Thee damn ah-doktor does not know ah-*what* could be causing her vizhion problems, bella. That is hiz *prob*lehm, capeesh? No clue, thees doctor."

Mom's not laughing. "Sure," she says. "It could be diabetes, or lupus, or Lou Gehrig's. I could have AIDS, or a brain tumor. I could be pregnant, for Christ's sake, and all these things could cause vision problems. For all I know, I could be in the early stages of chronic leprosy, and I think the doctor would still be clueless. Limbs could start dropping off before his eyes and still he would say, 'Hmm. Let's try yet another f**ing test.'"

Oh, my God. Lou Gehrig's? AIDS? Why am I not sneezing, or twitching? I'm not sure what to say. "Is drinking sugar syrup a way to test for diabetes?"

"Yes, it's called a glucose tolerance test. I have been drinking nothing but sugar water for the past six hours—I've had to go back to the doctor every two hours to get more blood taken to see my sugar levels. I haven't gone into a diabetic coma so far, which I assume is a good thing. If I don't get a hamburger and french fries pretty soon, though, I'm going to smack that doctor upside the head and *then* we'll see who's comatose."

My father just keeps rubbing, rubbing her lower back. "At least he doesn't think she has MS."

"MS?"

Uncle Pasta takes the giant book from Mom and hands it to me. It's her *Physician's Desk Reference*, which she uses to look up ways to kill off unsavory characters in her books. "MS stands for multiple sclerosis," he frowns. "It's a central nervous system thing—can affect vision, walking, sensory stuff. A lot of people end up in wheelchairs, or blind."

"But the doctor doesn't think she has that, thank God," says my dad. "Her spinal tap showed none of the markers for MS." And still he rubs and rubs, like maybe he can snuff out this negative mojo.

I sit in the space my uncle had vacated. "A spinal tap? You mean, he put a needle in your *spine*?"

She nods. "A big goddamned needle, and now I have a big goddamned headache."

Oh, my God. She's sick. I think she's really sick. How can she be sick? She never even sneezes or throws up or goes to bed in the middle of the day like everyone else I've ever met. She can't be sick. I would know if she was. My body would tell me —it would.

"Well, doesn't he have any more ideas on what to look for? Couldn't it be something more minor, like a migraine or something? I don't twitch or sneeze at migraines, and they can affect your vision." *Yes, please. A monster migraine, and that's all. Not Lou Gehrig's and not AIDS and not anything bad.*

I lean my head on her shoulder, trying to think of something that would comfort her. Something that would comfort me, because even my troll status in this family doesn't change the fact that she's my mother.

She is my mother.

I strain to think of something, anything to say that would lessen the tension. "I don't think you can have 'chronic' leprosy." I speak, still resting my head on her shoulder. "Stuff either falls off or it doesn't."

And when she kisses the top of my head I know it was the right thing to say, rehearsed or not.

"Well, we'll figure it out somehow," she says. "Daddy's going with me to get my last blood draw, and then I think we're going to stop and chow on something really disgusting, full of *trans* fats. Will you and Peter be able to scrounge something to eat?"

"We'll be scrrrrumptious, dear sister!" my uncle says grandly. "Ciao, bella. And Michael, ciao, bello."

Mom kisses us. Dad sort of waves and exits with his head down. He walks to the car with a hand on Mom's waist, gentle, like he's worried she might break. *He's really freaked*, I think. And watching my uncle leaf through the medical book, lips turned down almost to his chin, I think *him, too*. We're all freaked, and what if something is really, seriously wrong? I don't know what any of us would do if we lost her.

Shut up, Harper, I say to myself. *The doomsayer vibe is doing nobody any good. Why don't you bring the superhero version of yourself to life and find whatever is hurting your mom? Then squirt that supernatural mojo out your nose and vanquish it.*

Yes, self. That's a good idea. In the meantime, stop making things worse by having some sort of meltdown.

"So, Uncle Peter. How about pizza? I'll order it."

"Sounds scrumptious, dollface. I'm going to call Charles while we wait."

"Tell Charles I said hello," and we hug each other so hard I think we both might break.

☉☉☉

After a pizza dinner with silence as the main course, I head upstairs and log on to the Internet.

"Multiple sclerosis: an autoimmune disease that affects the central nervous system—the brain and spinal cord."

I wonder for a second why the names of diseases aren't capitalized? I'd think a disease name would equal a proper noun. But of course, there's nothing proper about them, just sucky, scary fearmongering emotions. Maybe that's why—they don't deserve the capital letter.

I continue scrolling down until I reach symptoms: "It can cause problems with muscle control and strength, vision, balance, feeling, and thinking."

Thinking? That's the way she makes her living. She can't have that—I won't allow it.

Sure, because trolls are in charge, didn't you know? This is the most helpless I've ever felt, because I can't even sense that something is wrong.

Not to mention Cora and the twitchy knees thing. My senses don't mean squat.

She doesn't have MS, remember? The doctor said her spinal cord fluid doesn't have the right markers. Remember that.

I look up some other equally hideous things for which she's being tested, and none of them make me feel any better. Pregnancy would be her best bet, but since she doesn't have ovaries anymore, that's out of the realm of possibility, supernatural mojo be damned.

Maybe I should be taking an ignorance-is-bliss standpoint on something besides the size of my pores.

After two hours of "looking things up," I just feel worse. I'm staring at a picture of a liver that was attacked by lupus when Mom knocks on the door.

"May I come in?"

"Of course."

She comes and sits behind me on the bed. "What are you looking at?"

I click the picture off and shut the computer down. *Never mind. She doesn't need to see that.* "Nothing, really. I'm trying to prepare myself for the next section of cat parts. I'm supposed to be getting all fired up about breaking the poor kitty's jaw tomorrow, I think." I turn to face her on the bed.

She's smashing my purple decorative pillow in her fists. "Eeeuw. I really wouldn't want to be in your shoes. Can't you get your partner to do it?"

I wouldn't want to be in your shoes either. I wish we could all get new shoes. "No, my partner is Larson McCready. I'm never going to be able to get him to do anything for me, because he thinks I'm an idiot."

"Oh, I'm sure that's not true. You're beautiful and smart and funny. If he doesn't love you now, give him time. He'll learn." She sets the pillow down and gathers me in her arms.

I bury my head in her shoulder. "Why is it moms can't see what everyone else sees? I mean, you're sweet and all, but it's super clear I'm the biggest dork. I think I have this special power but it doesn't do anything good and therefore isn't even an *un*special power. I love this beautiful basketball player and I didn't even know his season doesn't start till November." I feel the hives blooming. "I can't . . . I can't. . ."

She strokes my hair. I feel about six years old. Maybe four.

"I happen to think your mother sees you perfectly, and

everyone who really knows you does too. You, however, don't see yourself too well. That will come, though."

"What did the doctor say?"

"Well, I don't have diabetes. We still don't know what is going on, but we'll figure it out. We'll deal with whatever it is."

I lift my head to look at her. I'm trying so hard not to cry, and when she meets my eyes hers are bright, like she's trying not to either.

"Mom, I'm scared."

"Me too, Harper Ella Southwood. Me, too." She kisses me and stands for a hug. "It'll be OK, I promise."

I hope so. Please, in the name of all that's good, let it be OK.

I'm not religious, but if there were a time to pray, this feels like the time. I try to remember the words to some sort of prayer, but I finally give up and just ask the universe like five different times to take care of my mom and of Cora. I curse myself for not telling her about Cora and the cutting, and then I curse myself for thinking that way, because I don't want to add to the crap Mom's already going through. I go to bed feeling completely oogy and discombobulated. I think it takes another two hours before I finally drift off to sleep.

ʕ•ᴥ•ʔ

An insistent ringing wakes me up. *What the . . .* it's my cell phone. The clock radio says 2:00 a.m.

"Hello?"

"Harper? It's Joseph Perkins."

"Mr. Perkins? What's wrong?"

"Cora's in the hospital." His voice catches, and I can tell he's been crying. "Harper, she tried to kill herself. She won't talk to me—she won't talk to anyone but you. Please come. Harper, please come and talk to her."

11. Outsider

outsider /out'sīdər/ n. a person who does not belong to a particular group.

◊◊◊

In hysterics, I wake my mom and dad, screaming about how Cora is dying and it was all my fault. They practically have to slap me to get me to calm down, and all I can say, over and over, is "My knees, my knees. She was sick in her emotions, and it showed up in my knees. What kind of twisted power shows up in your knees? That didn't help at all. It's not like she couldn't walk. Oh, this is all my fault."

Mom holds me in the back seat, and just keeps shushing and stroking my hair, saying "It's OK. It's all going to be OK," while my dad drives Mach 10 to get us to the hospital. He keeps looking in the rearview mirror and running one hand through his hair, and I don't know if he's thinking about Cora or about Mom.

During the drive, I explain how I found out she'd been cutting, and about our fight and the gift of her mother's bracelet. When I talk about that, Mom's lips get all tight and I think, *That was a clue, wasn't it? That was a clue Cora was going to do this terrible thing and I couldn't even see it—I just thought, "What a beautiful gift," and tiptoed off into the tulips like a starry-eyed moron.* Oh, I should have told Mom about the cutting. She could read me the riot act right now, but she doesn't. Just strokes my hair and shushes me and tells me it'll be all right.

☙☙☙

Mr. Perkins sits on a couch in the waiting room with his head in his hands. There's another man sitting there, a more muscular version of him. That must be the uncle. When we arrive, Mr. Perkins looks up long enough to point upward and makes a number two with his hand—second floor—and my parents sit down opposite the two men while I walk across the room. When I reach the elevator, I turn to look back at my mom.

It's going to be OK, her eyes say.

The nurse at the station on the second floor gestures me to the room across the way. I crack the door to peek inside. Cora lies in a bed in the middle. Her eyes are closed and her arms are crossed over her chest like a vampire in a coffin. Each of her wrists is swathed in white bandages, and some red has seeped through.

Oh, Cora. This is the worst kind of cutting. What's the matter? What could be so bad you'd want not to live anymore? Why couldn't I help you? I'm so, so sorry. I can't even breathe, I'm so sorry.

A redheaded woman in scrubs sits at the far corner of Cora's room. As I peek, she alternates between reading a magazine and glancing over at Cora. *Oh, my gosh. They have to watch her. Cora's on suicide watch.* I feel like a giant hand is smashing my heart.

I push on the door gingerly, and her eyes open. Her beautiful green eyes have darkened to an olive drab, close to the same color as the circles surrounding them. Her hair is dark and limp, her skin pale, and I am just so glad she is there and alive.

"Hi," I say.

"Hi," she says.

What do I do now? "Your dad says you won't talk to anyone else."

"No, I didn't think I could. I'm not even sure I can with you, but you're my best friend. My best hope."

Jesus. I'm her best hope? I don't know how to do this. This is all my fault and I can't fix it. "Can you tell me what . . . I mean, why would you? . . . What made you feel . . . How can it be . . ." Jesus.

And suddenly I run to her bed, lay the side of my head on her chest, and the tears come like rivers. "Cora, Cora. My sweet friend Cora. You always do everything you can to help me and listen to me and comfort me and bolster my spirits." The tears are dripping onto her hospital gown. "And what do I do? I yell at you when you're in such pain it makes you hurt your own-self and then you don't tell me what's wrong—you never tell me what's wrong and then you try to kill yourself and I can't . . ."

I straighten. "That bracelet was a goodbye gift, wasn't it? You were planning this all day and I never had a clue, and I can't believe I didn't see it." And then I'm wailing, whining like I did while explaining the junk I said to Larson, but how stupid was that—sounding as hopeless about a stupid boy as I feel right now that I have almost mortally failed my friend.

"Oh, why do you even want to talk to me? I've failed you." And I lay my head back down and sob. I can feel her bandaged hands on my back, patting, patting.

"You haven't failed me, chickadee. I've failed myself. I have all this crap going on, and I just felt like I couldn't take it anymore. The cutting wasn't doing the job anymore." She picks my head up and scooches over on the bed so I can sit down next to her.

I sit, and grab her hand, but then I remember the bright-red lines seeping through the bandages on her wrists. I try to

pull away—I don't want to hurt her, but she grabs me back and holds on tight.

"Remember I told you the cutting didn't really hurt?"

I nod.

"Well, that was a lie. It hurt a lot. But at least I was in *control* of that pain. It wasn't caused by anyone else, and that way I could control it." She says all this while squeezing my hand so tight and staring away from me at the bathroom door. "I just wanted to control the pain."

"Why were you in pain, Cora? Who caused you pain? Was it someone at school? Your father? Who hurt you? Please tell me, and I'll do everything in my power to make it better." *I will help you, Cora. Just please, please don't do this ever, ever again.*

She turns her head to face the ceiling and closes her eyes. The tears squeeze out like small drops of rain from a pale cloud, and she shakes her head. "I'm not ready. Will you please just sit here with me until I fall asleep? I'll tell you later, when I'm ready."

"Of course. I'll stay as long as you want."

"Thank you. That's all I want." Her voice is fading. "It won't take long, I'm sure. They gave me all sorts of drugs."

She mumbles incoherent things for a few minutes, and I watch and hold her hand until her mouth falls slack.

Cora, please let me help you.

She's folded her bandaged hands back up over her chest and under her chin, and she looks like a little girl. I stay and watch over her until I'm absolutely sure she's asleep.

Then I walk out of the room, into the waiting arms of the best parents a troll could ever have.

12. ABuSe

abuse /ə byōoz/ v. treat (a person or an animal) with cruelty or violence, especially regularly and repeatedly.

ᓍᓍᓍ

I don't get home until about four Tuesday morning, and somnambulate back to my room, unable to speak or articulate what Cora had said. Which was nothing, really. When I open my eyes the clock says 10:15. I guess my mom must've turned off the alarm.

Oh, no. I have to go to school. I throw off the covers in a panic, but then the door opens.

"I called the school and told them you weren't going to be in today," says Mom. "I thought you might want to go back to the hospital and see Cora. Do you think you'll be OK without cat dissection and Larson?"

"I think cat dissection and Larson will be just fine without *me*, at least. I didn't want to break the poor kitty's jaw, anyway." I look at her. Her hair is a disheveled mess down her back, and she's once again in a T-shirt and Dad's underwear. She looks like such a teenage girl, and she certainly doesn't look sick. "How are you feeling today? How is your vision?"

"It seems better, actually. I think the doctor wants me to have an MRI today, though. Another Goddamn test." She waves her hand dismissively. "Ppphhhhttt. I don't think there's one thing wrong with me that a Caribbean vacation couldn't cure. Peter agrees."

"And what does *Dad* think? And what's an MRI?" The way she is blowing this off is typical Isabelle-girl-power attitude, and still I'm worried.

"Dad thinks I should do whatever the doctor says, of course. So I'm going to get the MRI, but only because I want an insider's view of my brain. MRI stands for Magnetic Resonance Imagery, or Imaging, or something like that. You probably never heard of it because no one you know's ever needed one. It basically means they use magnets to take cross-section pictures of my brain. It sounds like a living autopsy—taking out my brain via the computer, chopping my gray matter, and fanning the slices out like liver pâté, to see what's in there. Only the plate is the computer screen, and the crackers . . . well, the crackers are what shoots my nifty little metaphor all to hell."

"Do they then print out a sheet, like an X-ray photo, of your brain? That could be the cracker." Mom trying to downplay the intensity of this by joking doesn't alter my realization that something could be seriously wrong, especially if it's necessary to cut her brain into slices, metaphorically or not.

Why didn't my stupid body give us any warnings? I could've at least been preparing. Dealing. I don't really know how to deal with this.

"Mmmm." Mom sits next to me on the bed. "Did Cora say anything last night? About why she did what she did?"

I shake my head. "No, she said she wasn't ready to tell me. She cut her wrists, Mom. It was like when she cut herself before, only now she did it in the worst place possible. In a fatal place, even." I stare down at my Pinewood High shorts, which I slept in. "Mom, why would she do something like that? What could be so bad that she would want not to live anymore?"

"I don't know, sweetheart. The truth is no matter how hard you try or how much you want to, you will never be able to fully understand what goes on in another person's head, or in their lives for that matter. I hate to say the stereotypical thing that suicide is a teenager's permanent answer to a temporary problem, but often that's the way it plays out. Something is going on with Cora that she doesn't know how to fight or how to stop, and she just took the only way out, as far as she could see."

"I'm a teenager. I think. And I can't imagine anything that would make me want to kill myself."

She slaps my knee for emphasis. "Exactly my point! Life in your head is obviously not the same as life in Cora's. You don't have to understand it, honey. Just be there for her and support her. Don't judge her."

"I keep going back in my head trying to figure out what I missed. I mean, I know she must miss her mom. But she's been dead for a few years. Why now?"

"What about her dad? This whole year you've been friends, and we almost never see him and she's always here with you. Do you think he's hitting Cora?"

I lift my knees and slam my feet back down on the bed, like that's gonna help me understand. "No. I really don't. She never acts scared of him or seems uneasy around him. Just . . . disappointed, I guess. Like she gave up on him a long time ago."

"I'm worried, too, honey, about what might have gotten Cora to this point." She strokes my hair. "Just keep listening."

I hug her. "You're so smart."

"Awww, shucks." She pushes my shoulder a little and I fall back onto my pillow. "I've just been on the planet *ever* so much longer than you. I can't help absorbing a little more information. Now, take your shower and go on—be a rock for your friend."

ⓈⓈⓈ

The hospital looks exactly the same in the light of day. I'd thought that the terrible fear and the darkness of 2:00 a.m. were what gave it the aura of pain and stress, but nope. It's there in the fluorescence of the morning, too. I guess the building knows: people are sad here.

When I poke my head into Cora's hospital room, her eyes are closed, but her face looks sad anyway.

When she opens her eyes and her gaze meets mine, it isn't sad so much as . . . lost. "Hey, chickadee," she says softly.

The rest of the room is empty. "I see your watcher is gone."

Cora's eyes travel to the corner. "Yeah, the doctor was here talking to me for, like, a long time this morning. He's decided I'm not a threat to myself any more, I guess."

"How do you feel?"

She holds her bandaged wrists up to the air. The bandages are pristine white and new, with all traces of blood hidden securely under gauze. "Other than supremely stupid, you mean?"

"Don't feel stupid. Just talk to me. Do your wrists hurt?"

"Surprisingly, not too much. I'm just so tired. The doctor said I lost a lot of blood, and he was glad I didn't cut in the other direction, or I would have died for sure."

"The other direction?"

She demonstrates with her damaged hands. "You know, I cut from side to side. If you cut longways, from your palm down toward your elbow, that's a major artery and you bleed out really fast." She looks down and speaks to her chest. "I knew that, actually."

I shuffle in to sit next to her. "What happened, Cora? Please let me help you. Please tell me."

She shakes her head. "The problem is, there is no solution. I don't want to tell you because there's nothing you can do about it. No one can."

If I straighten one leg so it stretches out on the bed, I feel like I'm closer. "Well, maybe not. But I'd like to try. I'd like to listen, anyway. Maybe just talking about it can help you not want to break out the razor so much." I pet her shoulder, and then stop. *She's not a dog, stupid.* My knee twitches once, then is still.

Cora's head stays down and she keeps talking to her chest. "My mom is dead, you know."

"I know. I don't know how I know that, though, because you never talk about her or what happened to her."

The white-bandaged hands start rolling back and forth, like separate creatures. "Her name was Amanda, and she was beautiful. We used to have so much fun when I was little, all three of us—my dad, too. He wasn't always like he is now, you know? Is he still out there in the lobby?"

I shake my head.

"She got breast cancer when I was seven, and she fought it and beat it and then it came back again. She fought it again and beat it, but then when I was ten it came back again and this time it was everywhere—in her lymph nodes, in her blood and bones. Everywhere." The wrapped hands roll faster, like a frantic conductor. "She spent two more years fighting her heart out, but the cancer won. I was twelve when she died." Her hands finally slow, and come back to rest on her thighs.

"I'm so sorry, Cora." *But why do you want to die now over something that happened four years ago?* I want to ask, but I don't. I remember the other day when I spilled my guts full of judgment all over her, and how hideous I was. *Just listen, stupid.* "I can't imagine how you got through that."

"The second time Mom got sick, my Uncle Luke moved in to help. I was eight years old at the time."

"Is that your dad's brother? The one who was sitting with him last night in the lobby?"

She scoffs, and the hands below the bandages curl into fists. "God, was he here? Of course he wouldn't show his face in my hospital room. Bastard." She presses the heels of her palms into her eyelids and starts rubbing furiously. I'm afraid she'll bruise herself, or open her cut wrists.

"What did he do?" I start to reach under her forearms and bring them back down, then I stop. "Did he hurt your mom when she was sick?"

She removes the violent hands, and her eyes blaze. "No, but he could have. He kept coming into my room the whole time my mom was sick, and he kept telling me that if I told her, it would kill her quicker. Bastard."

"He . . . came into your room at night? Oh, God. He . . ."

Oh. My. God. He molested her. Cora's uncle molested her. She was only eight years old. And now he's back.

Cora sits up in the bed. Her hands have lost their power, and they fall, defeated, to rest on the mattress. Her eyes well with tears. "He raped me. All the time. Well, not all the time. For the first month or so, he came and just sat with me. He held me and we talked about my mommy and we both closed our eyes and we wished and prayed out loud that she would be OK, that the cancer would go away. We created stories where the cancer was, like, this evildoer like Lex Luthor and I was the superhero who vanquished it. Or he was. Or we both were—like a superhero team that killed cancer. Then the hugs turned to touches, the bad kind." Her breath hitches into a kind of hiccup, and she stops.

"Cora, I . . ."

"No, let me finish. I have to finish telling you. It has to

come out, somehow, or I'll have to cut it out."

"I'm sorry." *No more cutting anything. Please.*

"There are the bad touches, ya know? And he starts telling me that the bad touches are really good, that they help his superhero powers and that will help my mom. And it just gets worse and worse—he keeps touching me and making me touch him and saying that we're helping my mom. When he started raping me and I told him I didn't think that could help my mom, he kept insisting I was helping his superhero powers, but that if I told her the powers would go away and Mommy would die." She looks at me, and I try to tell her with my eyes that I'm listening. I don't want to interrupt again.

Then she looks away again. "After about a year, if I would say anything to him about it, he'd just say 'Your mom's gonna die.'" Another sob and hiccup. "'Your mom's gonna die.' He raped me until I was eleven, then he lost interest." She shrugs. "I started getting boobs when I was eleven, and my period started, and he lost interest. That was the year my mom wasted away the most, the year before she died. She couldn't talk to me about getting breasts, or about getting my period. Or about getting raped by Uncle Lucas."

She throws her arms around me and that's when she completely loses it. She cries like a wounded animal.

I can't believe this is happening. This happened. I can't believe this happened to her. "I'm so sorry, Cora," I mourn. I place a hand on her shoulder. "Sweetie, chickadee. I'm so sorry."

"How could he use my mother's cancer to keep me quiet?" Her voice sounds like it's coming from the bottom of a well. "How could he do that? Why would anyone do that?"

"I don't know. I just don't know." My knee has been quiet since she started talking, and I wonder if it is because her sickness is out in the open. My body doesn't need to warn me that something's up with her, because now it's out there. "Why is he here now? Couldn't you report him now? What about after she died? Did you tell your dad?"

She laughs, and the laugh sounds more like a bark of pain. "Oh, I tried. About a year or so after she died I tried to tell him, but we were in the middle of a huge fight, and I blurted it out. He said I was just trying to hurt him, that he knew how much I loved his brother and that I was being a real bitch for trying to hurt him."

"He said that?"

"He did. Like I told you before, he's not the same as he used to be. He was great, a great daddy before my mom died. But he's just been so angry since then. He's mad all the time." She sniffs and wipes her eyes. "He's been happy since my uncle's been here. Bastard."

I grab her hands and hold them, careful of the bandaged wrists. "Your uncle needs to be punished, Cora. He needs to go to jail. He's a pedophile and a rapist, and he needs to go to jail."

She lies back wearily. "I don't think I can do anything about it now. It's too late—he hasn't touched me in five years, and if my dad doesn't even believe anything happened, why should anyone else?"

"I believe you, Cora."

"Well, of course you do, silly. You have to. It's like a . . . what do you call it? For being a best friend. A pre-*rutchamaw-hooey.*" She pats my knee with her gauze-covered hands.

My mouth involuntarily curves up. Even now, in the midst of this . . . this evil, she's funny. "A prerequisite."

"Right, a prerequisite. You have to." She closes her eyes, and I can tell she's getting sleepy. "I don't think anything can be done now. I just have to suck it up for a couple of years till I can move out." Her voice is getting quieter. "I shouldn't have tried to kill myself." I need to lean in to hear the last sentence as the words fade away. "I should have just been patient."

I sit with her until I'm sure she's asleep. I don't think she should just wait out her time in that house. Lucas Perkins needs to pay. I feel like I'm jumping out of my skin with desperation to find a way to help her. We can make him pay.

It's lunchtime. Mom had said she'd come back and pick me up in the afternoon, so I detour to the nurses' station for a phone book. I take it and my cell phone into a lobby in another section of the hospital—labor and delivery—and settle down to start making phone calls.

13. Test

test /test/ n. a procedure intended to establish the performance, quality, or reliability of something, especially before it is taken into widespread use.

ⓥⓥⓥ

"**Did you know** there is no statute of limitations on criminally charging sex abusers of children?" I plop down in the passenger seat of Mom's Honda.

"Good grief. What did you two talk about in that hospital room? Were you watching Court TV?" She peers at me over sunglass lenses.

"You know, I can hardly wait to get my driver's license. I'm going to go make an appointment with Child Protective Services, and I think I would look more like an adult who means business if I drove there myself."

I see the hospital fade from the back window as we pull away.

"Maybe I'll drive to the police station and see about filing charges there. Go straight to the source—you know, the guys with the handcuffs and guns. Of course, it's only September and I have two months until my birthday, and that's too long to wait. I have to go now. Or, maybe tomorrow since it's after five now. Of course, the police station doesn't close, it's—"

"Stop! Breathe. What in the world are you talking about? Filing charges against whom?" Mom's hand moves to the gear-shift, and instead of heading home she shifts down to pull into a strip mall.

She turns the ignition off and faces me. "Go."

"Do you remember that man who was sitting next to Cora's father in the hospital lobby? That's her Uncle Lucas. He molested her until she was eleven, and used her mother's cancer to keep her quiet, and that's why she tried to kill herself, because he's back, and he's such a bastard but she thinks it's too late to make him pay and no one will believe her, but I believe her and Mom, we have to go and have him arrested!" I bounce up and down on my seat like a little kid begging for candy, but it's justice I'm begging for. For which I am begging. Whatever.

Mom's eyes well with tears. "My God. That's horrible. Poor Cora." She shakes her hands, like she's flinging sludge from her fingertips, then wrings the knuckles like an elderly woman. Uncharacteristic of her, to look so helpless, but I know how she feels.

Where can we go from here?

"I knew it would have to be something major to get her to that point," she says finally. "She's so strong."

"Let's go! Let's get that dickhead, and get justice for Cora." I reach over and turn the key, and Mom's little Honda roars back to life. OK, it sputters, maybe chugs. But it's running, and I'm ready.

Mom puts her hand on my knee. "I know you want to help your friend. But it's the end of the day, and there's really nothing more we can do for her right this minute."

"But—"

Mom raises a finger to shush me. "She's still at the hospital, so she's safe. Tomorrow, I think you should go back to school. I'll be glad to follow up for you with the police or Child Protective Services." She pulls forward on Seventh Street, heading east toward our house.

No! No going back to school. Let me do something on my own. Something brave for Cora. I can calm the chaos that led her to pick up the razor. I must find a way to help. Please. "Mom. Do I have to go back to school? I really feel like this is something I can do myself. I don't know if I can face Larson and the cat dissection."

"You know how I feel about your missing school. You've only been a high schooler for two weeks now, and I don't want you to start the year with a lot of absences. The further you get in your education, the harder it gets to catch up on things you've missed." She stops at a light, turns and winks. "And I'm sure Larson was devastated without you today." She seems a little recovered from the news of Uncle Lucas. Maybe because we have a plan.

I don't know, though. My heart hurts for Cora, plan or no plan. "Har har. I'm sure Larson didn't even notice I was gone, what with the love affair between him and our dead cat, whom he named Spike. He was way too excited about Spike on Monday."

Mom continues, "Anyway, I'm sure your math class did something you will need to make up, and keep up on. I know you want to ride to Cora's rescue, honey, but I think maybe CPS might take an adult a little more seriously, especially since we're not relatives of Cora. We're outsiders, and it could get a little dicey."

As we pull up to our house, I can see Uncle Pasta's and Dad's cars already parked.

"I don't know *why* they would take an adult more seriously," I feel like I'm grousing, but she's not listening like she should. "If they're supposed to be protecting children, you'd think they would listen to children first." I jump out of the car and almost stomp to the door. I feel thoroughly eviscerated, like Spike on the table, stripped of my guts and my ability to act.

My uncle and my father are opening the door as I approach. "Well, how did the test go?" my father asks. He looks beyond me to address my mother, who is slowly exiting the car.

The MRI. Of course, I forgot about the MRI and jumped right onto whatever issue was front and center in my own solipsistic little brain. I'm such a selfish brat.

"The test was fine," she says, "if you enjoy spending time holding your breath in an iron box while a really loud machine ratchets in your ears and takes magnetic slices out of your brain."

"I'm sorry, Mom." I turn to meet her as she comes up the walk. "I totally forgot about your test."

"Well, what did the doctor say?" asks my dad. He holds out his hand, grabs Mom and leads her into the house, where Uncle Pasta sits on the edge of the couch, waiting anxiously.

"There was no doctor there—only a technician. He was very nice, helped me pick a radio station and gave me headphones, then turned it up as loud as I wanted to avoid the horrible noise of the machine, and I think he had Xanax or Valium or some other downer all ready to give me in case I had an anxiety attack in that metal bubble thing I had to go into. But he said he couldn't read the scan. It had to go to the doctor who'd discuss it with me at our next appointment—which is Monday."

Uncle Pasta jumps from the couch, and my dad's eyes catch fire. "Monday! You have to wait until Monday?" he barks. "That's ridiculous. They need to tell you right now. They can't leave this kind of test just flapping in the wind. They can't leave people . . ."

"What? Wondering for another few days?" Mom says. "I'm pretty sure it's not a life-or-death situation. It'll wait. Besides, we have things to do this week. We can't be worrying about stupid brain-slicing scans. We need to worry about Cora." She reaches around Dad, shoves at Uncle Pasta with her butt, and pulls me onto the couch with her. "Now CORA, Cora is in a life-or-death situation. I think we should concentrate on helping her." And she proceeds to ignore the shocked looks from her brother and her husband and launches into Cora's story.

I can't believe I forgot about her test. She really doesn't look too worried. I'm not sure how she does that.

14. Voluminous

voluminous /ve'lyoomənəs/ adj. occupying or containing much space.

✺✺✺

"OK, Mom—are you sure you're feeling OK? Sure you don't want me to stay home and talk to the police about Cora?" I really don't want to go to school today anyway. I feel a lack of participation in Lucas Perkins's arrest would be a letdown to Cora. A letdown to *me*—I promised I would help her.

"No, honey, I really want you to keep up at school. I'll text you later; I promise."

I sigh and try not to look too much like I'm pouting. I clear the breakfast dishes as slowly as possible, in the hope she'll change her mind before I have to leave. I balance my cereal dish in the top rack like it's a priceless sculpture and look up. Her crossed arms and her look say she ain't buying it. I position my spoon in the middle of the silverware rack and look up, again. Plaintively, from under my eyelashes.

Nope, isn't going to work. Damn. I blow out my breath in a whoosh. "OK, but I'm telling you—if Ms. Haglione runs me to death or Spike comes to life and kills both me and Larson mere minutes before we were to have our first kiss—I'm holding you responsible."

She places my backpack over my shoulder while steering me toward the front door. "I accept the responsibility. And if Ms. Haglione or Spike kills you, I will stop at nothing to avenge your death. Because I love you. Now go."

The elderly *tai chi* foursome is a twosome this morning, man and woman inching along in sync. I wonder if these two are a couple—they almost seem joined together.

I wonder if Larson McCready and Harper Southwood McCready could be this great, everlasting, eternal couple sixty years from now, so comfortable with each other it seems like they are one. I like that.

☾☾☾

Acting is busy already this morning. Kids stand in groups, talking and stretching. One girl has both hands wrapped around a foot pulled against her butt, and she yanks at that quad and arches her back. The whole scene is like something out of one of those reality TV shows like *So You Think You Can Dance*, or *Dancing with the Stars*, which I know about only because Uncle Pasta watches them. He says it's because he simply loves to watch dancing, but we all know it's a bit more about the muscular men in leotards and spangly costumes.

I walk up to Cade Castell, who's standing with a slightly less enthusiastic group, watching the others—circus goers checking out the side show. Or maybe the monkey act.

"Hey, what happened while I was gone?" I ask. "It looks like opening night at the Met."

He fingers an eyebrow piercing. "Oh, we had like an hour-long treatise on the importance of warming up. Acting is athletic, and dangerous, didn'tcha know? And now we're rehearsing for a scene. We're doing it today."

"We're doing a *scene* today? Did you have to memorize lines? How did you memorize lines in one day?" *Oh, God, I knew I couldn't do this class without Cora. My head is going to explode right up there on the stage in front of all these New York Broadway-show wannabes.*

My panicked look must be glow-in-the-dark, because Cade reaches over and grips my shoulder like he's the last branch at the cliff's edge. "Hey, it's chill. There are no lines. No English or any other language, actually. We have to do the scene in Gibberish. Remember? According to Bakener, we cheated at this the other day."

This other Goth guy in the group says, "Yeah, we have to do our scene at a restaurant, where there is some kinda conflict. Our scene is at a really nice restaurant that doesn't want us as customers. Doesn't seem like too big a stretch, ya know? Don't panic—you can be the hostess. Or the busser. What do you wanna be?"

I want to be elsewhere. I want to be taking care of Cora, or having her uncle arrested, or taking care of Cora by having her uncle drawn and quartered.

I settle for being the busser, and all I have to do when the fight breaks out between the patrons and the waitress is say, "*Nyah he ring ma hepneh dawhh,*" which is supposed to be Gibberish for "I'll clear the broken dishes when you're done throwing them." Or something like that.

Anyway, of course the patrons win the fight and the snooty restaurant is annihilated or forced out of business or has to skulk off in disrepute, or whatever, and Goths and outcasts everywhere are vindicated.

It's actually pretty fun and I can see why Miss Bakener digs the activity, if her goal is just to get us up there working on the emotional tone of our voice. We are supposed to be ignoring the language and "feeling the message that the words convey."

    I don't even throw up while I'm up on stage, and I think my emphasis of the word "*hepneh*" conveys an appropriate concern for the dishes. When we finish, the rest of the class applauds, and I sit down with my group feeling less troll-ish than usual.

ⓖⓖⓖ

I still feel OK during Ms. Haglione's PE class, because we're doing these fitness stations arranged in opposing corners of the gym, which means her yelling only permeates one section at a time. The rest of the time we can just count and jump, count and jump to the beat of our own private drummer.

    Plus I get a text message from Cora, which is easy to read and answer even though we aren't supposed to have cell phones in class. You'd think someone would have thought of that before designing gym shorts with huge pockets that little teeny phones can slip in and out of almost invisibly.

    "How's school?" says my phone.

    "WYWH" I text back, which means "wish you were here." I think?

    I really don't understand the language of texting, and I don't text very often because I'm always spending too much time spelling things out. I really would rather just spell words out, and I think if we're not careful, someday we're going to lose the capability of speech altogether, then *everything* will be gibberish. DYT? See, does that mean "don't you think?" or "do your thing?" Or . . . "dirty yellow toenails"? It's just annoying.

    Her text comes back. "Ditto. RU in class with Larson yet?"

    I shake my head, like she can see me, then I remember to text. "No, that's two periods away. Thank God, not ready for him."

I was typing "not ready for Spike, either," when Haglione the hag screams across the room. "Hey, Southwood! Are you doing lunges or scratching your butt? Let's go, Pokeymon."

I quickly press "send," slip the phone into the lifesaving pocket of volumosity, and start lunging away. Is that a word? Maybe voluminousness? I'll have to look it up later, but right now I'm just thankful for that big ol' pocket.

ⓞⓞⓞ

Algebra requires no real concentration today, as Mr. Thompson simply hands out worksheets and tells us to figure them out for tomorrow. Which is good, because the guy sitting next to me is getting sick and I'm fighting sneezes the whole time.

I spend the time contemplating: What *possible* good could it do to have advance notification, or worse yet, late confirmation, of someone's illness? The itch in my knee didn't do anything to prevent Cora's suicide attempt, and I've received no clues as to what, if anything, is wrong with my mom. It just has no purpose.

Useless troll powers . . . my only forte. I am useless.

15. ReSCue

rescue /'reskyoo/ n. the act of saving or being saved from danger or distress.

◎◎◎

The bell comes too soon and I have to gather my sneezes and my contemplation and ride the wave of fellow students who don't seem to realize I'm flowing toward my doom. Toward cat desecration, but worse yet, toward totally reliving my most embarrassing moment.

Toward Anatomy and Larson McCready.

Mr. Wolfram's Hawaiian shirts seem to get brighter and more colorful every day, and I wonder if he just gets more and more excited the further we delve into the innards of the cat. Euw. He's talking to someone at the far end of the room, and when my gaze travels to the other side, to my table, it lands on Larson. I suck in a breath—he is so beautiful, even in his apron and with his hands dipped in entrails.

What should I say? Should I make a comment about my premature basketball wishes, just try and blow it off? Should I pretend I never said it? *Should I curl up and die right here in the doorway, so I never even make it to the table?*

My vote is for curling up in the doorway, but then somehow I'm already at the table. *Here we go.* "Hey. What'd I miss?"

He barely glances up. "Oh, hey. We broke ol' Spikey's jaw. Crrrrack!" He pokes his fingers into the cat's jaw and twiddles its parts, presumably showing how malleable it is now that he'd shattered it singlehandedly. "You missed a great time."

"Hmm. Sounds like. What are we doing today?" *God, he's so cute. I guess I can be on board with cat dissection if it's something he enjoys so much.* "Ummm, I'm really excited."

Mr. Wolfram claps from the front. "Okee dokee, artichokees! Let's do a little surveillance of your kitty's cardiovascular system, kiddos. Today, we're going to open up the thoracic cavity—exciting! We'll get acquainted with all the gross structures inside these spaces—pun fully intended!—but do not take any of them out. Leave them in place for now: we'll do specific organ dissections in later classes. Let's just expose everything for now to get a general lay of the land.

"So, with your cat's ventral side up—that's the belly up, kiddos—make an incision along the entire midsagittal line—that's an anterior-to-posterior incision right along the midline, from the base of the neck to the base of the pelvis. Then make a second incision perpendicular to that first incision, paralleling the lower ribs—that's roughly where the diaphragm lies. And then . . ." Mr. Wolfram continues excitedly, and his energy becomes electric and his Hawaiian shirt fluoresces with the lab lighting.

"It'll get tougher because, to expose the thoracic cavity—that's where the heart and lungs lie—you'll be cutting through the rib cage and the sternum. It's OK to cut these. Don't worry if you tear the diaphragm—it's almost unavoidable. Just make sure to cut deep enough to expose everything but not too deep

that you damage the organs underneath. Call me over if you have questions or need help, OK? Get to it then."

Larson grabs the scissors and snips them through the air, his eyebrows bouncing up and down in rhythm. "Cuttin' through the rib cage, yeah yeah! Cuttin' through the sternum too, ooohh ooohh." He starts dancing around, snipping the scissors with every "yeah" and "ooh."

I'd like to say I joined in on the fun, but I just don't have the nerve. He can still look cool while doing a tango with surgical instruments, but I'm pretty sure I can't.

Suddenly he stops. "Hey!" he says. "Didn't your friend try to off herself last night?"

I'm stunned. "No, it was Monday . . ." *Wait a minute. That's none of his business. Of all the insensitive, careless . . .* "I don't want to talk about it."

"C'mon, Harper, what happened? Did she take pills? Cut her wrists? Inquiring minds want to know."

I can't believe he's saying this. I look around for help, and catch Mr. Wolfram's eye. My panicked face must have shone all the way to the front of the room, because he's at my side in a flash, parking himself in between me and Larson. "Can I help you with something, Harper?"

"Umm, yes, please. I'm afraid we're going to slice too far, and get into the organs." *And I'm afraid this man I'm going to marry is kind of a jerk. Just immature? I hope that's it. . . .*

"OK, let me show you. We're almost to the heart, and you don't want to slice into the heart, do you, Harper? Do *you*, Larson?" Mr. Wolfram glances over to me, and winks. He takes the scissors from Larson and starts deftly working them through Spike's outer layers. He leads us through the procedure until the bell rings, and he keeps Larson talking so I can escape and dive into the sea of bodies flowing down the hall.

Bless you, Mr. Wolfram.

◉◉◉

When I get to Mrs. Carstead's class, she has us work on a paper we had apparently started the day before. I lay out my notebook, my textbook, and my pen, and then I proceed to stare blankly at them all. I don't really see the point of being here, considering how not invested I am in my education right now.

I feel the vibration from my phone, and I hope it's Cora again.

It's my mom: "The police are going to want to talk to you."

I start to text a reply when a buzz in the room pulls my head up. A cop walks in and I think, *The police want to talk to me right this minute? OK, good. That's good. Let's get this show on the road.*

I text my mom: "They're here now," and before Carstead gestures my way, I start toward the head of the class.

16. OUTCRY

outcry /'out krī/ n. a strong expression of public disapproval or anger.

ⓞⓞⓞ

"**Harper, this is** Officer Lenox. He would like to talk to you?" Mrs. Carstead ends this with a question, as if asking, *Harper, what did you do?*

I shake the outstretched hand of a high schooler *pretending to be a police officer*—at least that's how old he looks.

"Hi, Harper. Tom Lenox. D'you think your teacher would let you out of class for a while to come talk to me?"

He has the cutest Southern accent, and my immediate and unbidden thought is, *Wow, Cora just HAS to meet this guy!* And then, *Oh, duh. She probably will get to meet him, but how will she be able to focus on how cute he is under these circumstances? I'm such a dope.*

Officer Lenox has short honey-colored hair and a deep tan over the kind of ropy muscles a mountain biker has, and I think he keeps shaking my hand longer than he would have, mostly because I'm not letting go like I should have. "Pleased to meet you, Officer." I look at Mrs. Carstead. "Mrs. Carstead, may I?"

"Of course, Harper. Are you all right? Is everything OK?" She pulls at her Princess Leia cinnamon bun. Her overalls are pink today, and she looks like one of the kids from the class, except for the circa 1977 hairdo. She also looks concerned, and I wonder if she's heard about Cora.

"Everything will be OK, if I can help it. If Officer Lenox, here, can help it. Right, Officer?" I smile, and can't figure out why I get *less* nervous and feel *less* of an urge to practice what I'm going to say when I'm around adults. Let Larson smile at me like that, and I'm a mute moosh pile. Or worse yet . . . well, we've all seen what happens when I don't get to practice.

"Right, Harper. Ma'am, if you don't mind. Harper will probably be gone for the rest of the period. Is there anything she needs to take with her?"

"No, she knows her assignment. And this is the last period of the day, so she can stop at her locker and get her stuff." Mrs. Carstead squeezes my hand.

I don't have anything to get out of my locker, since I've paid virtually no attention to my assignments all day.

Officer Lenox and I thank her on our way out. I'm conscious of the stares of the class as we exit, but no one shouts "Are you gonna cuff her, or what?" which is kind of what I was expecting. This one guy, Jeremy, would never have let the opportunity pass him by, but he was probably ditching today. He ditches most days.

Officer Lenox and I walk down the hall. Senior students who have last-period release are scattered throughout, and I wonder if he thinks they are the ditchers. Of course, I don't know for a fact that they are seniors. They could be ditchers.

"Do you need your bags?" he asks.

"No, I've got everything I need. Do you want to go to the library? We could talk there."

He looks surprised. "No, we're not staying here. Didn't

your mom tell you? We're meeting her at the RMCFC."

"RMC . . . Real Men Can't . . ." I shake my head. "Never mind, I'm no good at acronyms. Where are we going?"

"The Rocky Mountain Center for Children. Your mom tells me you want to do an outcry for your friend Cora, and I'm goin' to do the interview. They have an interview room and video set up there 'specially for this purpose."

"An 'outcry'?"

"That's what it's called when someone reports child abuse and wants to follow through with bringing a child molester to justice." From him the word sounds like "chahld." "That is what you want to do, isn't it?"

"Oh, yes! Cora's uncle did horrible things to her and she tried to kill herself when he came back into the picture. He has to pay for what he did. Can an outcry from me, a person who's never even *met* him, do that? Can I really help throw him in jail?" *Oh please, please, let this be something I can do. I never feel like there's anything I can do.*

He nods. "You betcha. There's a lot you can do, but I need your mom to be there when I tell you all about it, all right?" ("All raht" is how it sounds. Cute.) "So we're all on the same page and all the legal stuff's covered. Sound good?"

I nod so hard I almost disconnect at the neck. "Sounds great!"

We're coming up on his police car, and he walks around to open the door for me. I'm glad he feels the need to be a gentleman and not the need to push my head down to keep it from bonking the roof of the car. I wonder if that head push could become a habit? But I don't ask him.

I also restrain myself from asking him to turn on the siren, although it's difficult. Instead, I watch the streets of Pinewood fly by, and I think about Cora and picture Officer Lenox cuffing Lucas Perkins and then making sure he *seriously* bonks his head on the way in.

Rocky Mountain Center for Children is in a house, one of numerous Victorians sprinkling downtown Pinewood that has either been converted into trendy businesses like day spas and Pilates centers, or split into too many small apartments.

When Officer Lenox and I walk in, I see it looks kind of like a daycare center inside. Children's books fill a long row of shelves and scatter across a few short tables, and a plastic wagon full of toys snuggles in the corner of the room.

"Hi there, and welcome!" The woman behind the front desk stands and extends her hand to me. "I'm Louisa Tripoli. Hi, Tom, how're ya doin'?"

Louisa Tripoli is smaller than my mom, even, and has shorn, spiky red hair of the type that, before today, I'd have thought looked good only on magazine models. She has a smooth china-doll face, except for a long scar that starts at her right temple, sort of bisects her eyebrow, and puckers her eyelid. It makes her look sarcastic, you know, how when people raise one eyebrow and put a hand on one hip to look down at you. Her smile is genuine, though.

"I'm well, Lou-Lou," says Tom. "Thankfully, it's been over a week since I've been here." He looks over at me. "RMCFC has another function besides outcries. It's also a shelter for battered women and children. They come here to escape a situation of domestic violence and have a place to stay while they figure out where to go next."

I glance around. "And there's nobody here now? That's good."

They both laugh. "Right now we have six moms and ten kids here," says Louisa. "They're in another part of the house. It's not visible from the street; we bring them in through a secret entrance in the back. You'll see one or two in the office occasionally, but people don't know there's a shelter here. We keep a low profile."

I really don't understand *anything* about what other people go through, do I? "How do you keep the husbands from finding out? Couldn't I just go home and tell someone about what this place really is? Not that I ever would. I mean, I never would. Ever. Of course." *Shut up, Harper.*

She shrugs. "Sometimes we don't keep husbands from finding out. The women sign a confidentiality agreement. Your mom already signed one and there's one in your paperwork, too—that usually works. They don't want the husband or boyfriend to find out where they are. Usually. But it's tricky psychology, abuse. Sometimes after the fear has had a chance to die down a little, women remember they love their significant other, or they just get more afraid of what will happen if they don't contact them, so they'll try. One of the worst scenes happened before I started working here. I remember it all too well. I thought he was going to kill everyone on the whole street, and finish up with me."

She and Tom look meaningfully at each other. "I remember, Lou-Lou," he says. "That was a bad scene."

I'm confused. "I thought you weren't here at the time?"

She shakes her head. "No. I said I wasn't *working* here. I came to the shelter to get away from my boyfriend, and then I got stupid and called him." She touches her forehead, and my knee gives a violent twitch. "I'd barely even finished bleeding when I called him and begged him to come and get me."

How could you do that? And they still let you work here? Why would you stay with someone who did that to you? I have so many questions, but they all seem inappropriate. Then I remember what Cora told me about Uncle Lucas and how he kept her silent. But she was just a kid and this is a grown woman. How could she stay with someone like that? How . . . ugh. *Shut up,*

Harper. I need to work harder at understanding. And not being so judgy. Obviously. "I'm sorry," I say.

"'S OK." She strokes the scar, almost like she's drawing comfort from the rough texture. Maybe she is. "Hey, we could shoot the breeze for hours, but your mom is waiting for you. Tom, I have the camera set up if you're ready."

He straightens up, and I swear if he were wearing a hat, he would tip it. "Born ready, ma'am. Let's go cry out."

Louisa takes us down a long hall that seems like it wouldn't fit in such a small place; then I remember the six women and ten kids hiding out somewhere in here. Not such a small place, after all. We reach a door at the end, and she knocks. "Isabelle?"

Mom is sitting on a couch, reading a book I'm sure she's brought with her. She isn't into magazines and always keeps the latest thriller jammed into her purse for any wait time. Right now it's the latest Dean Koontz, and she dog-ears a page before setting it down. "Hi, Louisa! Hi, honey. Hi, Officer Haven't-Met-You-Yet. I'm Isabelle. Louisa, all the paperwork has been signed—it's on the table."

Officer Lenox shakes hands with Mom. "Tom Lenox, ma'am. Thanks for comin' on such short notice."

Mom's face lights up. "Ooh, a Southern police officer right here in the Mountain West! Where're you from, Tom, and may I use you as a character in my next novel?"

I'm not kidding: he actually *scuffs his foot*, head down, blushing, while giving a classic "aw, shucks" gesture. "I'm from Bella Vista, Arkansas, Mrs. Southwood, and I'm here in the Mountain West only because they transferred me here. I don't think I'd make much of a character to be writin' about—least ways, not a very interesting one." ("Interesting" comes out "inner-resting.")

She shakes her head. "Oh, I'm sure I'd beg to differ. Every life is an interesting story all on its own. But let's do this later, shall we? Right now I think we should start pursuing some justice for Cora and getting that Lucas Perkins out of her house and out of her life."

"I agree," Louisa says, and she hurries over to the camera, which stands opposite a small rectangular table that sits in the corner of the room. She motions me over, and without meaning to, I reach up to smooth my hair. My left hand almost slaps the right one back down. *You're not screen testing for a movie, idiot!*

Feeling foolish, I sit. "So, Officer, what's the procedure here?"

He sits in the other chair. "We're just gonna talk, Harper. You tell me the situation with Cora, where she is and how she got there, and what she told you about how she got there. That's all we need for now. At some point, you may need to testify to what you know in court, but . . ."

"What if he denies it? How can you prove it when it happened so long ago? I mean, there's probably not any physical evidence anymore, right? Like semen or scratches."

Isabelle calls from the couch. "Can you tell *somebody's* been watching their crime dramas on TV?"

Now it's my turn to blush and scuff my foot. "I just thought . . ."

Tom pats my hand. "No, you're right. Unless there's scarring, unless he was extremely violent with Cora, there won't be much in the way of physical evidence. And he's already denied the accusation. We asked Lucas and Joseph Perkins to come in to the station today—they were there at lunch. Lucas said he never did anything to his niece and Cora's father pitched a fit about how she was just trying to hurt them, and . . . it pretty much went the way it usually does."

Stress crawls up my belly and flushes my neck. "So he might not even get charged? They can't let her out of the hospital if he's still there, if he's still on the loose. They can't!"

"Now, I didn't say they wouldn't do anything," Tom interrupts.

100

"Based on your outcry, we should be able to remove him from the house, and he'll be forbidden to go within five hundred feet of Cora. This charge is a serious one—more serious than your average abuser, because he was an 'adult in a position of power.' Meaning he was responsible for Cora's care while the abuse was taking place.

"We'll gather as much information as we can. Then it will be up to Cora. Her testimony is what will prove the abuse took place." He has a pen out on the table, for taking notes I guess, and he rolls it back and forth under his fingers.

"How will her testimony prove it? Couldn't she lie?"

"Sure, anyone can lie. But we have experts in this field. There are certain consistencies, certain patterns to abusive behavior, and with children of abuse, that can't be made up." He pauses. "Do you think she lied?"

I shake my head vehemently. "No, no. Of course not. I saw her face, and I know her. She's really secretive, but this makes perfect sense as far as *why* she's been secretive. She's really kind and generous and caring, and I know she's telling the truth."

"OK, then, let's go. Let's cry out."

Louisa has been standing by the camera this whole time, and now she pushes a button.

Officer Lenox transforms into a very official-sounding professional: "If you would start by stating your full name for the camera..."

I take a deep breath. "My full name is Harper Ella Southwood...."

17. Fear

fear /'fir/ n. an unpleasant emotion caused by the belief that someone or something is dangerous, likely to cause pain, or a threat.

૭૭૭

Sitting in the car with Mom on our way home, I watch the outcry at RMCFC rewind inside my head. We both are still wiping tears from our eyes as the true impact of Cora's ordeal sinks in. It was like I hadn't *really* thought about it since Cora told me everything—what she would still have to go through, the scary enormity of what she would still have to face, *to do*, before she could put it all behind her. I just reared up and burst out of her hospital room like a fire-breathing dragon wanting vengeance and flew through the halls on the wings of my indignation. To save her—without stopping to think about what I had just heard.

Addressing the camera and registering the concern on the faces of Louisa and Officer Lenox effectively doused the dragon's fire and left just the troll, wet, shivering, and horrified.

"After we have some dinner, I could take you to the hospital to see Cora," Mom says. "Sound good?"

We pass the 7-Eleven on Fifth Street and I remember a Slurpee fight Cora and I had there during the summer. "Mom? How do you get over something like that? Will Cora ever be normal, like with sex and men and things?" I shake my head. "I don't think there's any way she can. If I had something like that happen to me, and somebody I trusted violated me like that."

I think of Uncle Pasta and how much I trust and love him. I know he would never do anything like that, and even *thinking* about him as a predator throws me into a creepy funk. Like living in an alternate universe. *How can people be so, so horrible?*

"I don't know, baby. I don't know how, or if, you can ever really recover from something like this, but you're the perfect person to help her try. She has a great support system in you."

I can't mute the snort. "I am hardly a whole system. What she needs is a mother, and the unfairness of the world is demonstrated in a crystal clear way right there, because as we all know, her mother is dead. Not to mention I let several very obvious clues that she *needed* my support whiz right past my self-absorbed little skull. Then my body totally betrayed me by not giving enough clues or the right clues or . . . I don't know. Look what happened."

We turn onto Glad Mountain Drive, my street, and I fight the urge to snort again. We are not living on a happy hill, not when it is a place where sweet little girls get hurt and destroyed.

"I think you are underestimating your importance here, Harper," says Mom. "One person's support can be crucial. Oh, shit."

Two unfamiliar vehicles are parked in our driveway, but it doesn't take familiarity to identify the owner of the big truck with the large letters on the side that spell out "Perkins's Plumbing." Cora's dad.

God, I'm sure he's so pissed at me. He's probably here to kill me. The hives and the heat start crawling up my neck like caterpillars. "Well, we knew the police were questioning them this morning," I say, hearing the tremor in my voice. "He's probably really angry."

Mom climbs out of the Honda with a face that looks carved from stone. "He can be angry until the sun sets in the east for all I care, he just better not even be *thinking* about taking it out on my family. He's here to thank you for helping his daughter, or he's bounced on his ass."

She marches toward the front door, and I follow, the rabbit behind the lion.

Our living room is usually a large, open space with high ceilings and overstuffed furniture spread throughout. Right now, Joseph Perkins sits on the big loveseat with his hands itching to grip the armrests, I can tell, but the rests are too far apart. Uncle Pasta and a handsome brown-haired man sit in the middle of the long couch—must be the famous Charles—and though none of them is especially big, the room is cramped and bloated with tension.

"Isabelle and Harper!" says Uncle Pasta. His face is filled with fear. "Thank God you're here. Where've you been? I was . . . worried." He squeezes Charles's knee, and receives a comforting pat in return.

Joseph stands up from the loveseat and advances toward us. His brown hair is rumpled and going gray at the temples, and his salt-and-pepper eyebrows are knit together, furrowed in fury. His colorless gray eyes blaze. "I can't believe you corrupted my daughter into believing this bullshit!" he snarls. "My brother would no more hurt Cora than he would cut off his right arm! He took great care of her when my wife was sick, and now that Cora's gone off the deep end and tried to off herself, he's back to help us both. You're all just feeding a crap sandwich to this teenage drama queen who *used* to be my daughter, but now she's just . . . is just . . . I don't know what she is!"

Isn't that what Larson said? That Cora tried to "off herself"? What is up with these people, so rude and horrible and . . .

My mom stands straight, with hands on her hips, and her brow is also furrowed in anger. "Mr. Perkins, I don't know why you're here shouting about things you obviously don't understand."

"Understand?" he shouts. "You're right! I can't understand a single goddamn thing about this whole stupid f**ked up mess." His hands reach up to rumple his hair even further. "I can't understand why my daughter has turned into a bitch from hell who wants to ruin me and my family, and you people have just joined the party to help lay me out."

"You and your family?" Mom scoffs. "*Cora is* your family, you twisted little man, and what she needs now is a father who loves and supports her, not some high-handed, judgmental dickhead who doesn't know his ass from his elbow! A world-class douche who'd rather come here and scream obscenities at her friend, a friend who probably saved her life, than be there for Cora."

Oh, God, she's talking about me—I didn't save Cora's life, I probably helped her try and kill herself by not recognizing the signs she was giving me. Oh, God, Harper. Say something! Don't make your mom do all the dirty work here, stand UP to this guy!

"My brother is my family, too, and if you knew what we went through in Desert Storm . . ." yells Mr. Perkins.

Mom is shaking her head. "Oh, now we're hearing war stories? Your brother saved you from some Iraqi who had a bayonet against your belly and somehow that makes it OK that he sexually abused your daughter for three years while your wife was fighting for her life? You looked the other way because you *owed* him, is that your story? You're pathetic!" Her eyes flash and she moves toward him.

Do something. Do something. . . .

Mr. Perkins and my mother are almost nose to nose in the middle of the room, and he seems to swell, bigger and bigger the closer she gets. He looks like he's going to hit her, and Charles and Uncle Pasta stand, I guess ready to jump into the fray although I can see they don't know what to do either.

"My brother didn't do NOTHIN' to Cora! Don't you get it, you bitch? And if you don't call this whole thing off, I'll show you what's what, I'll . . ."

"You'll what, Joey? You'll show me who's in charge the same way your brother showed an innocent little girl, your *daughter*, with threats and intimidation?" Mom shouts. "You'll . . ."

Do something!

I step between them. "Mr. Perkins, please, we only want to—"

And he shoves me! He and my mom keep this laser vision stare between them as I go flying into Uncle Pasta and Charles. They try to balance me upright, and Joseph and my mom scream nose to nose, and the room closes in on us. Then the front door flies open as Joseph raises his hand to hit my mom, the same hand he'd used to shove me out of the way.

Michael Southwood stands in the doorway. His six feet five inches fills the frame and makes him look like a short-haired blond version of Thor, in khakis and a tie. He takes in the scene in the blink of an eye, and before Joseph Perkins's hand can come down, Dad hurls himself forward.

"What the hell is going on here?" Dad shouts, and grabs the offending hand to shove it back down. "How dare you raise a hand to my wife?"

He then takes both of *his* hands and shoves Joseph Perkins full force in the chest. "How dare you come into my house and raise your hand to anyone in it?" he roars.

As Joseph stumbles backward and falls into the overstuffed loveseat, my dad is on him, pummeling and pounding and shouting, "Huh? Huh? Huh?"

My mom runs over and tries to pull at his shirt, yelling "Stop it! Stop it, Michael!"

Uncle Pasta and Charles join in, all screaming at my dad to stop.

My dad probably outweighs Joseph Perkins by fifty pounds, and Joseph is cowering in the chair's stuffing, holding his fists over his face, trying to block my father's barrage of fists.

Dad just keeps pounding, the "Huh?s" developing their own rhythm, while everyone else shouts "Stop! Get off!" And the noise blends into the tension of the room, creating a living force that hovers over the entire scene.

I stand back, waving my hands in the air like directionless birds, and I want to shout, want to jump in, want to do something to stop it. I need the superhero X-ray vision and supernatural mojo that should be attached to troll powers. I want to see through the anger and the fury that shrouds the room, and get down to the hearts underneath, where I'm sure the supernatural mojo can make everyone see the most important thing. When we get right down to it, all everybody here *really* wants to do is help Cora. But all I can do is stand there, helpless and alone and scared and drowning in a room full of rage.

It's my mom who finally halts the fight. All of a sudden she pushes herself off of the group, holding her hands over her eyes. "Oh, God," she says. "I'm so dizzy." She turns her body toward me with her hands still covering her eyes. She sways like a willow, and I'm afraid she's going to faint. Then her hands come out as she drops to her knees, moaning, "I'm so dizzy." Then she throws up.

I rush to her and help her lie down on the Persian rug,

careful to avoid the barf pile. Dad and Uncle Pasta and Charles all extricate themselves from the mess on the chair and fall to the floor, surrounding my mom. I guess Joseph Perkins is still curled up on the chair, but I'm not sure. I don't really care, because my mother is lying there with her hands over her eyes repeating, "I'm so dizzy," over and over again.

Uncle Pasta nods to Charles and Charles jumps up and runs with his cell phone to the other room, dialing 911.

Then my mom takes her hands from her eyes, looks upward, and starts to cry. "Oh, God. You'd better call an ambulance. I can't see anything. Oh, shit, I can't see!"

18. CHaNGeLiNG

changeling /ˈCHānjliNG/ n. a child believed to have been secretly substituted by fairies for the parents' real child in infancy.

ʘʘʘ

The ambulance takes my mom away, and my dad rides along. The paramedic keeps trying to take care of his bloody knuckles, and he keeps shaking her off.

Mom was sick three more times while we were waiting, and she told us that every time she moved her head, nausea took over. Dad and Uncle Pasta had finally stretched her out on the couch, and Dad held her head still, wiping blood on his shirt before holding on. His touch was the only thing that seemed to curtail the nausea. She lay there waiting, hands covering her eyes, without saying anything. My dad just stroked her cheek and I could see the tears creeping out from under Mom's fists.

Nobody knows what happened to Joseph Perkins, because by the time Uncle Pasta and Charles and I huddled together to watch my parents get transported away, he was gone. The "Perkins's

Plumbing" truck was nowhere to be seen.

"Uncle Pasta, what do you think is wrong with Mom?" I hiccup as I watch the ambulance roll away. "I swear, I haven't been able to sense *anything*. Nothing's twitching or signaling me in any way. How can she be blind all of a sudden? How can she . . . can she . . ." And then I completely lose it. *How can she be sick and Cora be sick and everyone I love is getting sick and I can't do anything to stop it. I can't even feel it coming. I should be the one who's sick. Why isn't it me?*

"Shhh shhh, bella," says Uncle Pasta. "The doctors will figure it out. They will fix her."

"She doesn't even believe in doctors." I feel like the tears are coming too fast to stop. They drown the words, make them sound mushy and snot filled. "She doesn't think they can figure *anything* out. Clueless, isn't that what she said?"

He hugs me, and I feel Charles gently patting my back. "The doctors can probably figure out what's wrong," he says. "Just because she doesn't believe in something doesn't mean it doesn't believe in her."

I extricate myself from the group hug, and wave them both away. "Yeah, sure, that's profound. Can we please just go meet them at the hospital? I need to be with my mother."

I walk toward my uncle's car feeling just like the ungrateful under-the-bridge-type troll I know I'm being.

The emergency room at St. Mary's hospital is newly remodeled, and I guess it's supposed to look like a mountain resort. Forest green leather (leatheresque, at least) couches have nubby wood armrests that match the legs of the side tables, and the pillows have prints of deer shapes and mountain outlines. There's even an unlit fireplace, due to the ninety-degree September weather, that should spark visions of an Aspen après-ski party. Or something.

The couple sitting in front of the silent fireplace is teary and tense, squeezing each other's hands like they're holding on to the last branch at the cliff's edge. Even if there were champagne fountains and ice sculptures here, it's still obviously a place for the sick and the dying. It smells like a hospital, and as Uncle Pasta and Charles and I sit in one of the green couches to wait for news about my mother, it feels like one too.

My head rests on my uncle's shoulder, and he holds my hand in one of his and Charles's hand in the other. I can tell by the way he keeps rubbing the knuckles on my thumb and forefinger that he is way more agitated than his expression shows.

"I keep feeling," I say to his shoulder, "like I should have had some inkling that she was sick. I can foretell a person's cold when my nose twitches and a flu with a sneeze, and Mom's triggered not even a sniffle and she goes *blind*? How can that be?"

On the other side of Uncle Pasta, I sense Charles swiveling his head to gaze at me. I guess he doesn't know.

I keep talking to the shoulder, although I now direct my voice toward Charles. "I'm pretty sure I am a changeling, which is historically and mythologically an interesting thing to be, but not so much fun in reality. I can tell when people are getting sick, I guess, but I didn't see this coming, and I feel like it's my fault. Maybe I could've prevented whatever is wrong with her."

I straighten up to look directly at my uncle's new boyfriend. He's regarding me with interest, and his eyes are that ice blue that is so striking when paired with dark hair. His full lips make the term "pretty boy" something of an understatement, and I remember Mom ruminating more than once about the unfairness of the beauty of so many gay men versus sweaty, sports-fanatic, farting heteros. Oh, God, but now she can't even see to compare.

"*Why* do you think you're a changeling?" he asks. "Because of this sense you have? About sick people?"

"No, that's something extra, I guess." I shrug. "I don't know. I just . . . you know. I looked into a lot of other possibilities when I was younger, but troll seems to fit the most. Look at my family. They're all so beautiful and confident and I don't look like anyone or act like anyone around here. And I look at people at school and I'm nothing like any of them, either. Like Larson McCready is so gorgeous and confident and he never says stupid things like 'good luck in basketball' when basketball's not till November and he doesn't have to rehearse everything and . . ."

I hiccup, and realize I'm crying again. I hiccup again. "And he doesn't have to look everything up and I know Mom sometimes likes to look stuff up but now she can't *see* the dictionary and maybe I could have prevented it and . . ." At this point I run out of steam and can only finish with a deep, shuddering breath. *I can't believe I am sitting in the ER spouting nonsense to a man I just met. Will the madness never end?*

Charles and Uncle Pasta both look at me, compassion radiating from blue and brown eyes. "You have my hair," Uncle Pasta says, yanking at his kinky head. "If I let it grow for ten years or so I would have a glorious furry ponytail just like yours."

"Yeah, sure," I sniff. "The fact that we both could grow shrubbery on our skulls just guarantees a blood tie."

Charles reaches across my uncle's lap to grasp my hand. "Harper, I need to tell you something. It's important. I know we've only just met, but I think I have some insight to share."

I meet his gaze full on. "OK. Share."

"I don't know what the deal is with your sense about sick people. That seems like a really cool gift, an intuition, or something, to me. My mother has the ability to tell when the phone or the doorbell is going to ring before it does. No one ever knows how she does it or where it comes from. As far as usefulness, I don't know if it has any. But it's a really great conversation piece." He squeezes my hand.

Uncle Pasta is nodding his head so hard it might fall off, and he looks so happy. I'm so glad he's happy.

Charles drops my hand and changes position on the couch, pulling one knee up to face me more directly. "Now regarding your troll status, this is what I know: I have two sisters, both of whom are grown now. They, like you, felt isolated, alone, and out of place for the majority of their teenage years. My youngest sister, Kirby, who is not as precocious as you obviously are, but who is very intelligent in her own right, once came to me after two friends of hers had slighted her, and told me she felt removed from everything around her, as if she didn't belong anywhere or with anyone. She said she might as well sit alone at the bottom of the ocean.

"I'm five years older than Kirby, and was therefore old enough to be past all that teenage drama . . ." he grins, "At least I was past it enough for her to confide in me, and for me to help her understand how much of what she felt was true for all teenagers." He takes a deep breath. "She wasn't a troll, but . . ."

Uncle Pasta grabs my hand and reaches over to pick up Charles's too, and he shakes them both like we just won a prize-fight. "She was a teenager! See, bella, that's all it is. Teenagers feel outcast all the time; it's practically required. You were born to Isabelle and Michael. You've been here the whole time, I swear, and you're not a troll. And whatever sense or gift you have, you will figure out a way to use it to its best possible end. But you can't blame yourself for not foreseeing what happened to Isabelle, or to Cora."

I sit for a minute, digesting. I don't know what to think about what Charles said. Not to mention I still feel responsible for both my mom and Cora, troll or no troll, but . . .

"Michael!" Uncle Pasta jumps up when he sees my father walk through the massive sliding doors from the trauma room. "What are they saying? Where is she? How is she doing? Can she see anything? Is she still throwing up? Is she—"

Dad holds up a hand to stop the barrage of questions. "She's sleeping. They put something in her IV to help the nausea, and she fell asleep." His hand slides around his neck and squeezes it, and the circles underneath his eyes seem to have grown exponentially darker since he crawled into the ambulance with Mom. When I look at the clock on the far wall of the waiting room, I see that it's almost seven. I guess the three hours of stress from fighting with Joseph Perkins *and* watching your visionless wife get transported to the hospital and sitting in the emergency room waiting to learn—what?—is more than enough time to grow dark circles under your eyes.

"She still can't see," he says. "They took her to give her another MRI and now she's sleeping."

"The MRI can show what's causing her blindness?" I ask.

He shuffles to the couch where we had been sitting and collapses into it. "I don't know *what* it's supposed to do." He leans his head into his hands and speaks to the floor. "I don't know anything. The doctors don't seem to know anything. I'll probably get arrested for assaulting Joseph Perkins. And my lovely, lovely wife is blind." His voice catches on the last word, and I can't help but start watching the floor for tears to splash it.

My strong daddy doesn't cry. He is Thor, god of thunder. He can't be crying.

But he looks up, and he is.

The trauma-room doors slide open, and someone in a white coat comes toward us.

Dad jumps up, wiping his eyes. "Dr. Ammon."

Dr. Ammon is bald and short and built like a weightlifter, green scrubs straining over Arnold Schwarzenegger's biceps. Now how did he have time during medical school to create those? I wonder.

"Mr. Southwood," he says. "Will you come with me so we can discuss your wife's MRI in private?" He has the fairly high voice that often accompanies really muscular men and always makes me wonder if the muscles squeeze the voice box? Something I can look up, I guess, if I ever feel like looking something up again. Right now, I don't. Sometimes knowing things sucks.

Dad looks around at the now empty ski-lodge-wannabe waiting room. He looks at Charles, who has a comforting arm around both me and my uncle. "No, we're all family here. Just tell us."

Dr. Ammon nods. "Your wife has had a severe inflammatory episode in her brainstem. I've looked at all the results of the tests she took over the last few days. There were two small lesions in her previous MRI, and now this one has confirmed my diagnosis given the evidence of the new lesion. I'm afraid she has multiple sclerosis."

19. PRoGNoSiS

prognosis /präg 'nōses/ n. a forecast of the likely course of a disease or ailment.

🐳🐳🐳

No.

No.

This can't be. I wasn't warned at all. I didn't know at all, didn't feel anything coming. What did the dictionary say, DESTRUCTION of the central nervous system? Paralysis? It can't be.

"Are you sure?" I say. The rest of the room is struck dumb, staring at Dr. Ammon like he's the two-headed monkey at the freak show. "That's why she's blind? Is she always going to be blind? Does she know yet? What does it mean?" *Isn't this the disease that makes it hard for you to think?* Oh, God, here come the hives. I can feel the warmth crawling up my neck, and if I had a turtleneck I probably wouldn't use it because *my mother has multiple sclerosis!* Nope. It can't be that.

"She doesn't know yet," he says. "The antinausea medicine we gave her really put her out, and I had time to look over her MRI. There is about a quarter-sized lesion right in the middle of her brain stem, and that's what's causing her symptoms."

Uncle Pasta comes out of his trance. "I guess I don't understand. She has a lesion that just appeared in the middle of her brain? Is that like a wound? It wasn't there this afternoon and now it is? I'm totally confused. Is she going to die?"

"Here," says the Doctor. "Will you follow me? I'll show you her MRI, and explain it in detail. And no, she's not going to die." He gestures toward a hall labeled "Radiology."

Mute, we follow—lemmings toward the cliff.

We enter a small room, with an electronic setup on one side—computer monitor and keyboard, plus wires and buttons—and a wall-mounted light box on the other. Dr. Ammon leads us to what looks like high-tech X-rays hanging from the light box. These are the brain slices Mom was talking about—the brain pâté. Or is this part the crackers? I forget. I think my own brain might explode—chunks of pâté on the hospital walls.

"MRI stands for Magnetic Resonance Imaging." Dr. Ammon gestures to the pictures, "Very high-powered magnets can take cross sections of any part of the body to see it in a very detailed form. In this case the pictures are of the brain and spinal cord." He turns his back on the picture now and faces us, clasping his palms together like he's a professor ready for an afternoon lecture. "Multiple sclerosis is an autoimmune disease of the central nervous system."

He gestures to the image. "'Autoimmune' means for some reason the patient's immune system focuses on a particular body part and sees it as an outsider—a foreign invader. Then it does what the immune system is supposed to do—it attacks the invader. Only it's attacking an insider, you see? In this case, it attacks the myelin sheath, which is the insulation around most of the nerves in the brain and spinal cord, and destroys it."

"Does it destroy it for good?" This is my dad, speaking for the first time, I think, since the doctor's diagnosis. His lower lip is soft and tremulous, like a small boy on the verge of tears, and I can't stand seeing him this way. "Is she going to be blind forever?"

"And what else could happen to her?" asks Uncle Pasta.

"What causes this?" asks Charles. "More importantly, is there a cure?"

"Nobody knows the cause, and at this point there is no cure," says Dr. Ammon. "However, a whole set of medications has been developed in the past twenty-five years, which can help slow disease progression. It's not a terminal illness, but it can and usually does progress. The myelin sheath can regenerate itself—so hopefully, Mr. Southwood, your wife will regain her sight."

The doctor makes a circular motion around a white splotch on the film. "The permanent damage comes when the same area is attacked repeatedly, and scarring spreads to the nerve itself. There are many things your wife can do to manage her MS and any related issues that may occur in her future. Right now, we'll start by giving her an IV infusion of steroids—probably several over the next couple of days. This helps ease the inflammation and can help speed her recovery, if she is going to recover."

If she is going to recover?

My dad throws up his hands. "If she is going to recover? I thought you just said . . ."

Again, we all start talking at once, and really, the exploding head thing is mere seconds away.

Dr. Ammon sighs, and his professional persona slips a little as he waits for us to calm down. He pumps both hands up and down, and I think he's trying hard not to "shush" us. "MS is a complicated disease. Most people who have MS experience what we call relapsing and remitting, in which setbacks are followed by periods of recovery. This said, disease progression is different for everyone, although it generally takes time, perhaps even many years, for permanent nerve damage to occur."

We are calm enough now to just stare at him as he continues. "For some, though, the disease can be chronically progressive, which means every time there is an exacerbation of symptoms, the nerve itself is impeded and the damage is permanent. We won't know the type of MS Isabelle has until we chart her symptoms and her recovery.

"I'm very sorry. I know this is a difficult diagnosis."

Dad looks at me. "How are we going to tell her?" Then, to Dr. Ammon. "Why now? Why the sudden onset?"

"Again, there is much we don't know about the disease. My understanding is that she was involved in an altercation this afternoon?"

We nod.

"A highly stressful situation could precipitate it."

I stare at Uncle Pasta. *See?* says my mind and my face. *It's all my fault. I knew it.*

He shakes his head, and of course his face says, *It's not your fault*, because what else could it say?

"She should be waking up soon," says Dr. Ammon. "Do you want to be there when I give her the diagnosis? Everybody's different. Some people want family there for support, while others would rather be alone at first in order to assimilate. Would you like to be there?"

Dad shakes his head. "No."

Uncle Pasta and I both jump in.

"Michael!"

"Dad!"

"Don't you think she would want us there?" in chorus.

His head keeps twitching, no, no. "No, I don't want you to deliver the news to her. I think I ought to do it. I think she ought to hear it from me." He looks at Uncle Pasta and he looks at me, and we both know he's right.

"Let's go," I say, and now as we follow the doctor out of the radiology room and into the room where my mother sleeps, we aren't lemmings so much as . . . as much as eager children clapping to save Tinkerbell. Or maybe we're the wolves following the alpha male. I don't know, a good metaphor escapes me, but now it feels like we're going to my mother with purpose. With resolution.

ⓞⓞⓞ

When I see Mom sleeping on the emergency room bed, I flash back to Cora. Was that yesterday? No, three days ago. I think. Maybe four. A year's worth of events seems to have happened since then. As I look down at Mom's face—so pale, with her braid wrapped around her shoulder and resting on her chest—I wonder if I've started a snowball rolling down a hill that's turning into an avalanche. I hope not.

My father goes to her bedside and sits next to her, leaning over and enveloping her in his arms. She opens her eyes from beneath him and hugs him hard, and he stays with his lips to her ear for at least four minutes. Her eyes stay trained on the ceiling, and though I know she can't see the patterns of lights and wires that twist there, her gaze holds steady as she listens.

At one point her hands tighten on his shoulders, and I can see tears pooling on her lower lids and spilling down into her hair. She turns her lips to his ear now, and he nods, and she nods, and they hug like they're clinging to forever.

She is my mother.

20. Overwhelmed

overwhelmed /ōver'(h)welm d/ v. completely defeated.

∽∽∽

Uncle Pasta, Charles, and I duck out of the room to leave Mom and Dad alone. That hug made me feel like a trespasser. I think anyone would have felt like a troll there, regardless.

We stand in the cold hallway. "Well, I don't know what to do to help her," I say. "What do you think we should do?"

Uncle Pasta rubs my shoulders. "I don't know, bella. Why don't you wait a while and then ask her what she wants us to do?"

Charles chimes in. "Peter says you like to do research. Maybe you could find out as much about MS as possible and then you'll have lots of information at hand when she's ready to ask for help."

"I started to do that when she was getting all the tests. Then I got scared and shut the computer off. I couldn't read anymore."

I take them both by the hand and pull them back to the waiting-room couch we had occupied before. "Uncle Pasta, why do you think my special sense, or 'gift' as you call it, Charles, didn't give me any clues about Mom and the MS? It's really bugging me."

Uncle Pasta shrugs. "I don't know, bella. Maybe it's because you're just too close to it. You're so close to Isabelle, maybe that blocked your senses."

I shake my head. "No, I knew something was up with Cora, and she's my best friend. I didn't know what, I admit, but my body still sent the message." Then something occurs to me. "Oh my God, Cora! She's still over on the second floor. Mom and I were going to come and see her when we saw Mr. Perkins's truck. What should I tell her about Mom? What about what happened with her dad? And with the outcry?"

I clap hands to my ears, like that would drown out the noise that's accumulating in my brain. "I don't know how to deal with this all at once. It's too much, too much. I'm not ready, I don't know how . . ."

I start to cry again. "I just don't understand how all this bad stuff can be happening to all the people I love, and nothing's happening to me. How is that fair? I know, I know, life's not fair and blah blah blah yada yada . . ." I hiccup, "yada. I don't care. This is ridiculous. What if she never sees again? Before I turned that computer off, when I was reading, it talked about cognitive loss. What if she can't think to write her books?" I scratch and press at the deer shape on the couch. "And what if Cora's uncle goes free? She's been hurting for so long, and he's such an evil asshole." Another hiccup. "I can't stand it."

Uncle Pasta holds me. "I know it's not fair, bella. None of it is. All we can do is be there for them, and make sure they know we will do anything possible to help them. And they know. You're doing so much for Cora already. I know you don't feel like it, but you are." He gathers his fingertips together, kisses them, and splays them out. "You are *bellissima!*"

I just don't feel like I believe you.

"What my silly wannabe-Italian boy is trying to say," says

Charles, "is that we all just do the best we can in a crappy situation. Don't you believe things happen for a reason?"

"I used to, but . . ."

The trauma-room door whooshes open and my father comes out. He still looks sorta like he's been run over by a truck, but maybe now it's a smaller truck—a pickup instead of a semi.

"They're getting ready to move her to a private room, but she'd like to talk to you, Harper."

I stand and take a deep breath. "OK."

Uncle Peter kisses his fingers again, and lifts his hand to rest the fingertips on my cheek. "Go, Harper. Just tell her you love her."

ⓒⓒⓒ

I nod to the nurse inside the windowed admissions desk, and she presses a button to allow entry. Mom is in the third bed down, I guess it's called a gurney when you're still in the ER? The other two beds are surrounded by curtains covered in opaque geometric shapes, which is OK by me because I don't think I can handle blood and guts right now. I walk to the third bed and pull the curtain around us.

She is sitting up, with two or three more tubes attached to the IV sprouting from the crook of her arm. The machines behind her head are busy, with lines and lights and numbers doing their different things, framing her, a small sculpture of stillness, in the middle. She's staring straight ahead and using a thumbnail to push down her cuticles on the opposite hand.

I see her purse hanging from a coat rack that stands behind her, and the dog-eared book peeking from inside of it. It almost kills me. "Hi," I whisper.

"C'mere, honey." She pats the mattress, and I gingerly sit beside her.

What now? Should I hug her and tell her everything's going to be all right? She's so little and pale, I'm afraid she might break, and even though I know that's silly—she's really strong and I know she won't break and I just . . .

"I'm not going to break," she says, "and I really need a hug from my beeyootiful girl."

The tears gush again, and I practically collapse against her. "How did you know I was thinking that?" I sob. "I mean, you have these great muscles and it's not like they are just going to instantaneously disappear, but that's what I was thinking. And then I saw your book in your purse instead of in your hand and your *vision* instantaneously disappeared so maybe it could happen to your muscles and I could break you. And I'm so sorry this is happening to you and I don't understand *why* this is happening to you. . . ." I hitch a huge breath, choke on it, and start to cough.

She rubs my back as I lie against her. "Shhhh. Shhh. It's going to be OK. It's all going to be OK."

I straighten back up. "I don't understand how you can say that? You're lying here in a hospital bed and you're dizzy and you can't *see*. Aren't you scared?"

She nods toward me. "Shitless. Witless. Any degree to which I could be scared, I am." She's looking toward my face but not really *at* my face, which I find really disconcerting, because she's usually all about the eye contact. "I sort of knew, though," she says, "that this was probably what was wrong with me."

"*How* did you know?" I sniff. "Did you have a sense? Because I'll tell you, my senses in this case have completely failed."

She drops a hand on my knee and tilts her head against the pillow. "I learned from you and looked it up. Remember when I shattered that iced tea? Well, I've dropped several things over the past couple of months, so I did some research. MS seemed like the most likely explanation, although I thought maybe Parkinson's, too. But I haven't really been shaking, just randomly letting go of drinkware and flatware."

"So what . . . what are you going to do?" I couldn't believe it. Here we were all falling apart and she was comforting us, instead of the other way around. Well, no, that's not true. I can totally believe it.

She shrugs, "I'm not going to die, anyway. At least, not anytime soon. So that's the most important thing of all, don'tcha think?" Her eyes get a wet sheen. "All the stuff I read says there are several ways this disease can go, and most all of them are manageable these days, and you know what they say about that which doesn't kill you. Every day above ground is a good day."

I rest my head on her shoulder again, hugging her. "I'm so, so sorry. This sucks." *I don't know what else to say. This so, so sucks big time. How is she going to write?Stop, stop it Harper. Her vision is going to come back, I know it.*

"It sucks big time," she says. "But you know, some of the stuff I read, it said fifty years ago people used to treat MS like a death sentence, even though it technically wasn't. Doctors basically gave the diagnosis and then said, 'You might as well get in bed right now, because you're going to be paralyzed and bedridden before you can say "paralyzed and bedridden."' Can you imagine? WTF?" She squeezes me a little harder.

"Now, because of these new drugs and because they say that an active lifestyle is the best way to deal with MS—not that people shouldn't know that's the best way to deal with anything—now it's a lot better. A lot fewer people end up in a wheelchair, and those who do end up in one much later than they used to. So hell, maybe I'll be headed for a wheelchair in twenty years or so, and by then I won't need one because there will be a cure. Or because everyone will get everywhere they're going on cool space-age hovercraft."

"I vote for the cure, not the hovercraft."

She grins, and boy is that nice to see, even without the eye contact. "Me, too. Hopefully before I have to deal with any baloney like wheelchairs." She all of a sudden gets brisk and no nonsense. "Besides, everything happens for a reason, don't you think?"

"Uncle Peter's new boyfriend asked me the same question right before I came in here."

"Mmmm, Charles. Now how pretty is *that* pretty boy? Well, what did you say?"

I turn my head and stare at a green circle and blue square on the curtain. "I said I used to, but what could possibly be the reason for this? There can be no good reason for this, I'm sorry."

"Sure there can. Maybe I will be a test subject of some sort, and I'll be the one whose results bring about a cure. Maybe, because people know my books, I'll be one of those public figures who educate others about MS, like Michael J. Fox and Parkinson's. And by the way, I'm really glad I have this instead of Parkinson's or lupus or HIV, or some of the other BS they tested me for. For which I was tested, sorry."

"You could've been pregnant."

She chuckles. "Yes, the immaculate, ovary-free conception. I think that would make me much more famous than I am now, don't you agree?"

But I'm not ready to let this go. "What about Cora? You can't tell me her suicide attempt was meant to be—not to mention all the repulsive things her uncle did to her." I smack my hand on the side of her bed. The motion ripples the circle and square. "Much less the fact that her mother died this horrible slow death, and she was left without a mother. You can't tell me that all happened for a reason."

Mom shook her head. "You're right, I can't tell you that. But I still believe it. I think, not right now, but at some point in our future—Cora's and mine—we'll be able to come out on the other side and see a reason behind everything that's happened to us. Have you seen Cora, by the way? Weren't we on our way to see her when Joseph Perkins threw in the monkey wrench?"

A couple of guys in scrubs—they look about my age—peek around the corner. "Mrs. Southwood?" says one. "Sorry to disturb you. We're going to transfer you to your room now."

They roll the curtain back on its track as I jump up and move out of their way. A guy comes around to each side of the bed, and they start rolling her gurney along with all the surrounding paraphernalia at the same time.

"Harper?" she calls as she's being rolled away, "Go ahead and see Cora, and let her know about the outcry and how she's going to have to testify."

I cross my arms, put my hands under my armpits, and sigh. This is all so crazy. "What should I tell her about you?"

"Tell her I'm going to be OK. And tell her her dad is understandably upset, but he'll come around. I love you, honey. Come back and see me later. The nurse told me these steroids are probably going to make it hard for me to sleep, so I'll probably be bouncing off the walls and in need of a conversation partner. Or hey, maybe you can read to me."

"I love you too, Mom." *I love you so much. I hope, I hope with all my heart that you're right, and that everything's going to be OK.*

As the wheels clack away, I hear her talking to the two guys. "You sound young. Are you nurses?"

One of them says, "We're CNAs, ma'am. Certified Nursing Assistants."

"Really? How interesting. I bet there's a story there. May I use you as characters in my next novel? . . ."

21. LiMBo

limbo /ˈlimbō/ n. an uncertain period of awaiting a decision or resolution; an intermediate state or condition.

◎◎◎

My dad and Uncle Pasta are hugging my mom as she's wheeled through the waiting room. She must've asked those CNAs to take her through there, because I'm pretty sure regular traffic wouldn't use that route.

How upsetting would that be? You're waiting for news of a sick loved one, and gurneys filled with screaming gunshot victims are rushed past you. It'd be like a bad reality show.

All three men stand and watch her go. I step between my dad and uncle and hug them both around their waists. "We had a good talk," I say. "She kinda knew already, did she tell you that?"

Dad nods. "Well, it doesn't really surprise me. She plays it all nonchalant, but she's not about to go into a situation like this unprepared. She's detail oriented, even though she plays the laid-back, que-será-será thing so well. She's tough and brutally honest with herself, and like I said, she wouldn't go into important stuff willy nilly. Not her style."

Uncle Pasta squeezes my hand. "You are like her in that way, bella. She likes to look everything up, to know all the answers. See, the apple really doesn't fall far from the tree, I keep telling you."

"Yeah, well, I know I couldn't take news like this and still be scouting out ideas for my next novel. Did you hear her talking to those nurses' assistants?"

He nods. "I remember when she was doing research for her fourth novel—*A Monster Born*? One of her suspects was a Pentecostal minister, so she conned her way into this tent revival where they did snake handling, remember? She almost got bitten by one of the snakes because she was being nosy, and as some of the church members escorted her out, she was still asking, 'So *what's* that phrase again? That one dinky biblical passage that makes you all risk your lives handling snakes on a regular basis?' Anyway, she could've been bitten, or arrested, or worse, but she had to experience it because she wanted her book to be realistic. There's no stopping Isabelle. And she's going to prove it, just you wait."

"Are you ready to go home?" asks my dad. "It's been an incredibly long day for everyone. And Harper, you need to go to school tomorrow."

"No! No school, pleeeeeaase. I need to come back here and stay with Mom and Cora."

"The hospital is doing a fine job of taking care of Mom and Cora. And speaking of your mom, you know exactly what she'd say: 'No getting behind in school.'"

I huff, "There are millions of kids at that school who are gone days at a time. Weeks, even."

"Yes, and I'm sure their grades reflect that fact."

I turn a pleading face to Uncle Pasta. He shakes his head. "*No bueno*, babe. I'm not going there—I agree with your parents.

Let's go home."

I guess now's a bad time to play the pouty teenager. "OK, but we have to stay a little while longer—I still haven't seen Cora since the outcry. I have to go talk to her. Will you wait?"

My uncle strikes a pose and does a "swish" with one hand. Just for my dad, I'm sure. "OK. There'th a Gene Kelly double feature on TCM. We'll jutht cuddle up here in front of the ER television and enjoy it, right, Michael? Right, Charles?"

Charles looks at my dad's face and, thank God, doesn't join in on the swishy fun. He just goes over to the television set in the corner and switches it on.

My dad shakes his head at my uncle and nods his head at me, so I guess that's a "yes" and I can head toward the elevator. Toward my friend.

ଡ଼ଡ଼ଡ଼

Cora is up, her bed elevated and the television on.

I'm just not sure which things to tell her and which I should leave out until she's feeling better. What would I want if the situation were reversed? I think I'd THINK I'd want to know everything, but then once I knew it . . . I don't know.

"Hi, chickadee!" she says. "What's the word in the big city? How's Larson? Have you reeled in that juicy fish yet? Jeez, I bet I have a complete boatload of homework, and still . . . I really don't want to go back." She seems much more animated, and my knees, right now, are quiet. But the bandages around her wrists and the bruising under her eyes remind me: she's fragile. *What do I say?*

"Some things have happened, Cora."

She looks up at me, then down at her lap. "Things about my uncle?"

"Some about him, some about my mom."

"Isabelle? What's happening with Isabelle?" She sits up straighter, and I launch into a no doubt feeble attempt to break a mass of scary, awful news to her gently.

◎◎◎

The sky is dark on the walk to school this morning, and the clouds that tower over my neighborhood, threatening to spill their tears onto the trees, match my mood exactly. It wasn't that I'd come down the stairs and expected to see my mom at the kitchen table, because she wouldn't have been down there anyway. But the house had felt empty, and I knew school would too. The elderly *tai chi* foursome is nowhere to be seen, and I walk the street alone in the gloom.

Acting class is all sitting in the auditorium chairs when I arrive, which I don't understand until I see a substitute teacher who's a dead ringer for the Crypt Keeper on that HBO show from the eighties. He snail-walks among the rows, passing out worksheets on stage terms, and once finished, he doesn't say anything. I guess everyone is afraid he's gonna break into that cackle, because no one else says anything either. They just settle down to work.

Cade Castell sits away from the rest of the class, and when he sees me enter and take a seat far away, he gets up to bring me a worksheet. "Are you OK?" he mouths silently, because maybe even Goth guys are afraid of the Crypt Keeper.

I shrug my shoulders and don't want to meet his gaze because I'm afraid I'll start crying. So he goes back to his seat.

In PE, we do wind sprints back and forth from gym wall to gym wall, because it's been sprinkling and Ms. Haglione doesn't want her one-inch hair to get wet, apparently. I run with a fierce intensity and a rhythm that matches my thought processes until I think I might throw up.

Lucas Perkins had better go to jail forever and Cora's father had better figure things out or I am going to kill them both—touch the wall.

Whatever that thing is on my mom's brain had better start regenerating itself pronto or I am going to kill IT—touch the wall.

The mindless chanting works pretty well in Algebra, too, and I don't really hear anything Mr. Thompson says about whatever formula he's teaching us. But I guess I wrote it down, because when the bell rings, my notebook is covered in notes. *Maybe I can learn all this stuff subliminally, with my right brain, while I am plotting revenge against the world's evils with my left.*

Both sides of my brain shut down, however, when I walk into Wolfram's room and see Larson. I didn't think he was the type to get to a class early, but I guess if Spike was there . . . *He is* standing over our table, and Spike is looking like . . . well, like a science experiment gone amok.

A couple of Spike's body parts are already in jars which Larson looks to be arranging, and as he sees me walking toward our table, he gives me a smile that could melt metal. I almost forgot his insensitive remark from the other day. *Was that yesterday?*

"Hey, Harper. I think we get to tour the digestive system today. We're gonna take a trip through it just like little Spikey's food would. Sick, huh?"

"Sure, that sounds like a sick trip." I sound like such a dork when I try to use slang. Oh, well, worse problems.

"Do you want, like, the scalpel or the scissors?"

"Oh, you decide."

"I think Wolfram just put new blades on all the scalpels. You take that one." He hands me a shiny scalpel with that mischievous-boy, slightly-crooked-tooth smile. Wow.

"Thanks, Larson." And I settle next to him like we're an old married couple, playing Parcheesi (*how do you play Parcheesi, anyway? I'll have to look it up*) instead of carving up cats. My inner speech against Lucas Perkins and multiple sclerosis continues, but it's quieted somewhat by that little tingle I get when Larson's glove touches mine. By the time the bell rings, I feel like I might be able to get through the rest of the day.

22. PaTieNCe

patience /ˈpaSHəns/ n. the capacity to accept or tolerate delay, trouble, or suffering without getting angry or upset.

⊚⊚⊚

I open my eyes on Saturday morning and just lie there, staring at the ceiling fan above the bed as it whirs in never-ending circles. Mostly it's just a blur, but every few seconds the individual blades became visible, and I wonder if the fan slows down enough for that to happen, or if it's a trick of my eyesight. Probably it's some amazing thing that eyes do, and when mine blur with tears for the eight millionth time because my mother's eyes have gone dark and because Cora's eyes have witnessed such misery, the fan seems to stop and hang suspended.

I soak up the tears with the heels of my hands and look at the clock: 8:00 a.m. *I wonder if it's too early to go to the hospital and see them? I wonder if Joseph Perkins is going to have my father arrested for assault? I wonder if Larson is thinking about me?* I shake off this last thought right away. Stupid, trivial. *Why don't you quit filling your head with nonsense and think about something important? Why don't you*

DO something important?

I sit up and hug my knees to my chest. I can't think of anything important to do right this minute, except maybe feed myself. I guess that's important enough for now. I can't help anyone else if I collapse from hunger.

First, I go into my parents' room and put on my mom's Tweety Bird robe. It smells like fruit, because she wears this mango body spray. The smell comforts, but it also makes me hungry, so I continue down the stairs.

Speaking of robes and comfort, at the kitchen entrance I'm greeted with the vision of Uncle Pasta *and Charles!* at the table in their bathrobes. Whoo-ee. My uncle has never brought a boyfriend home. At least he's never brought one to the breakfast table. *I wonder what Dad thinks about this? Maybe they're getting serious. I hope so. Uncle Pasta SO deserves to be happy.*

"Good morning, bella. And how are we zis morning?" Uncle Pasta breaks out the faux Italian accent, which I take as a good sign.

"I'm OK. Is that an omelet? Hi, Charles."

From his seated position, Charles is leaning over his right leg. He looks up and smiles at me. *What is he doing?*

"Hi, Harper," Charles says. "Mmmm, yes. *Tamagoyaki* omelet —Japanese. Your uncle made it. He's a culinary genius, but he doesn't advertise it. Apparently that's your dad's territory, and I think Dad's territory is sacrosanct, correct?" He straightens his back, and pulls a needle from his thigh.

A needle?! What is going on? Is Charles doing drugs at our kitchen table? Over Japanese omelets?

And suddenly something stings my ear. I clap my hand to it and dig around. No bugs that I can find, but still it stings like something's biting it. I lean to the right and pound on my head, hoping to dislodge whatever's causing the pain. "Ow, ow. Oweee.

Something stung me. I thought all the summer bugs were gone? Charles, excuse the nosiness, but are you doing drugs at our kitchen table?"

Charles pops a cap on top of the needle, covering it, laughing. "I am, in a manner of speaking, doing drugs at your kitchen table."

"Charles has juvenile diabetes, bella," says Uncle Pasta. "He has to give himself insulin shots sometimes four or five times a day to regulate his blood sugar."

"Juvenile diabetes? But he's not a juvenile."

Charles laughs again.

Boy, everyone sure was merry on this morning of *my-mom-is-still-blind! Sheesh*. "I got it when I was a juvenile, though—it's called type 1. Type 2 is the kind adults get, and sometimes they can just regulate their blood sugar through diet and exercise."

"Oh, well, I'm glad you're not a druggie. But I'm sorry you have to give yourself shots. That must suck."

I walk around between the two men. Charles shows me the spot above his knee where the needle went in. I can't see anything there now.

He waves me off. "You know what they say: 'That which doesn't kill you makes you stronger.' I'm used to the shots."

"Yeah, Mom just spouted that cliché yesterday, too. You guys are all just so nonchalant and strong and gee, that must be nice." I shake my head. "I don't know why I'm feeling all sour grapes. I also don't know what was up with that stinging in my ear, but I guess it's gone now. Weird. Where's Dad?"

"Well, change-of-subject woman," says Uncle Pasta, "Your father is already at the hospital. I was waiting for you to get up so we could go. Are you to change out of ze robe or do you wish to fit right in wis ze patients?"

"No, this robe doesn't flap open to show my butt, so I wouldn't really fit in anyway. I'll get some clothes. Charles, are you coming?"

He shakes his head. "No, I think your dad has seen enough of me for now, and you guys need some family time. Thanks, though. Tell Isabelle I'm thinking of her. Cora, too, even though she doesn't know me from Adam."

"Will do."

ⓞⓞⓞ

The hospital is really busy this morning when we get there. Nurses scurry and patients meander but I don't see any doctors.

"I guess more people get sick on the weekends," I say to my uncle. "You would think it's just the opposite—weekends are the time they can relax and not get exposed to all the germs from work."

"No, but they get exposed to lots of beer drinking, partying, wrecking their automobiles, fighting with each other, and doing all sorts of things that would put them into the hospital." He smiles at an old man waiting by the front desk who's walking an IV pole with one hand while using the other to clasp his hospital gown closed.

"Ah, got it. Good point."

We pass one set of elevators to get to another. Mom's room is on the third floor, room 361. Second door on the left as you turn left off the Pike's Peak elevators, not the Rockies West elevators. This we know because of a very detailed phone message left by my father. This, we didn't really need to know, because about five hospital employees stop us on our way to ask if we needed help finding anything.

"Customer service," remarks Uncle Pasta. "Now, *this* is the place you really need it."

"Amen to that, Uncle." The door to 361 is slightly ajar, so I peek my head around. "Hello?"

"Come on in, Harper." My dad looks up from his position on the bed next to my mom, and gestures us inside. "Peter. We're having a lesson; come on in."

Mom is sitting straight up in the bed, and a nurse in brightly colored scrubs with a flower print sits in a chair on the other side of the bed. *I thought all scrubs were green? I must still be living in television land.* The nurse is holding an orange, and stabbing it with a needle. My parents are both watching intently. Mom *looks* like she's watching intently, at least.

"Mom, you look like you're watching that orange."

She looks up, right at me. I think. She smiles, and her color is so much better than it was last night. "I am! Sort of. My vision is still blurry, but I can see. Those steroids must really have kicked in overnight, because oh, glorious day, I can see!"

Oh, glorious day, she can see! "That's so awesome, Mom. What about the nausea? Are you still feeling dizzy?"

"Yes, some dizziness. No barfing, though. And my right hand isn't working so well." She lifts her hand to show me. "The doctor says that lesion really covered a lot of different nerve areas, so there's all sorts of symptoms associated with it. But right now I can see, and that's the greatest thing to be able to do. You can't imagine." She takes the orange from the nurse, aims the needle, scrunches her nose, and stabs the orange.

"What's with the orange, little sis?" Uncle Pasta navigates around the nurse to get closer to the action.

She pulls it out and puts her eye close to where the hole would be, then she gleefully stabs and stabs it, Jack the Ripper style.

We've never realized how much we love to see, have we, Mom? Time to celebrate with a little produce annihilation.

"I'm learning how to give myself injections," she says to us. "This is all great, with the orange and all," she says to the nurse, "but you want me to do this to my *leg*? I don't know about that. Michael, maybe you can do it." She looks at the now bent needle. "Just don't do it this way."

The nurse hands another syringe over, and takes the destroyed needle back to deposit it into a box on the wall labeled BIOHAZARD. "Yes, I want you to put injections in your legs, glutes, arms, and sometimes your stomach. You have to rotate the injection site every day, or you can permanently damage your skin."

I suck in a breath. "You have to give yourself a shot every day? You're kidding. What is that supposed to do?"

Dad takes the new syringe from Mom and watches the *accordionated* needle as it goes into the box. *I don't really think that's a word, but it seems appropriate for the damage that was done. A shot every day? That so sucks big time.*

"The neurologist wants her to start on one of what they call the ABC drugs right away," Dad says. "They're designed to help slow the progression of the disease. He thinks he should start with this one called Copaxone, which requires a daily injection. She might go to a larger dose and give herself the shot only three times a week, but for right now . . ."

Mom interjects, "This one has fewer miserable side effects. And you should see the big-ass needle you have to use for the *A* drug. Screw that, I'm not getting stuck with a piece of metal that looks like it wants to poke right through my goddamn leg, and out the other side. And the pills! Talk about a laundry list of side effects. Unh-unh. No thank you."

Uncle Pasta smiles and pats her shoulder. "So glad to see you back in your usual fine form, sis. I was worried."

"I'm still worried," I say. "I mean, I'm uber glad you can see again, but then you say your hand's not working well, and this whole MS thing is so scary. What kind of side effects?"

"Oh, some of the drugs can cause sickness or general

malaise for a day or so after the injection, or skin reactions, like the nurse said. The list is not nearly as long as, say, your average allergy medication: you know, side effects include the shakes, the faints, possible heart attacks, appendages falling off, blood seeping out your pores, death, that kind of stuff." She looks at my dad. "Michael, what about it? Do you want to give me my shots? On the days you have to do my glutes, you get to grab my butt, ya know?"

"Mom!" my fists clench, "Be serious, please." I'm getting upset. "You could end up paralyzed. I'm scared, and I don't know how to help you." I move up to the bed and push my dad, the orange, and the needle out of the way. I rest my head on her shoulder. "What if you end up paralyzed? Or you lose your vision for good, for real?"

She strokes my hair. "I know, honey. I'm scared too. But the fact that I have this disease is something that's beyond my control. All I can do is deal with what comes next. If I end up paralyzed or blind, I guess I'll have to get a wheelchair and a braille typewriter. Go ahead, be scared with me."

Her finger follows a curl around my ear, which isn't stinging, by the way, and I'm not sneezing or twitching or anything. I just don't get it. She stretches the curl and lets it pop back in.

"It helps to know the people I love care what happens to me and worry about me. But Nurse Emily here has been telling me lots about the progress they've made in treating this disease over the past twenty years, so let's just try and be glad I was diagnosed now instead of in 1950. Can you do that? Can you work on being glad this is happening now instead of then?"

I speak from my position on her chest. "I can try." *I can try being as brave as you are, but I don't know if I'll ever make it.*

She squeezes me. "That's my good girl. So Michael, honey, whaddya say? Shots for me?"

"Sure, I can do it," he confirms. "But what about when

I'm not around? What if you're on a book tour?"

Nurse Emily interjects. "They make an injector pen. You feed the needle into it, then push a button on the top and it injects the medicine. You don't even have to look at the needle."

Mom kisses my forehead. "See? There ya go. Problem solved. Now, Harper—tell me what's up with Cora."

23. influence

influence /'inflŏŏence/ n. the capacity to have an effect on the character, development, or behavior of someone or something, or the effect itself.

ⓥⓥⓥ

Mom finished her steroid infusions and her injection training by late Saturday evening, and we got to bring her home. We walked Mom into the house, then into her bedroom, where she promptly fell asleep. We soon followed suit. Cora was still at the hospital, which I think had more to do with my father than with her still needing to stay for medical reasons.

Dad had gone to find some bigwig administration muckety-mucks to tell them about the situation with Cora's father, how even though Lucas Perkins was out of the house, it still wasn't a good idea for her to go home. I'd asked if she could just come home with us, but then my dad started talking about legalities. Cora was still a minor and her dad was still in charge, and her upcoming court case and blah blah blah.

Of course, there was the teensy little matter of the fact that my dad had clocked Joseph Perkins right in the face, and we still didn't know if the police were going to arrest my dad, or what. All very *One Life to Live*, and if I weren't so emotionally involved in the tragedies, I'd find the situation a little humorous. A ridiculous, black comedy.

಄಄಄

So now everyone's awake, and sitting at the breakfast table like Beaver and the Cleavers. Uncle Pasta made *ebel-skeebers*—which was a word that I actually did look up, although I'm not sure when I did that?—for us, since Dad doesn't seem to be in the mood. Anyway, I learned they are Danish round pancakes called *aebleskivers*. I like Dad's word better, and since Uncle Pasta serves them with an Italian accent and an air-kiss, we call them *Italian* round pancakes named *ebel-skeebers*. So there.

"How are you seeing this morning, Mom?" I ask. "In my dream last night, all the steroids you took gave you X-ray vision like Supergirl. You spent your time rating the underwear of people on the street." I scoop some round pancakes onto my plate and cover them in powdered sugar. "Mmmm, Uncle Pasta. *Ebel-skeebers* rule."

"Well," Mom says, "I'm still blurry. A little better than last night, though. But I think the steroids are giving me Supergirl's circadian rhythms. I didn't sleep at all." She looks up at her brother, who's poised at her side with the skillet and the wooden spoon. "Did you know those are Danish round pancakes and they're actually called *aebleskivers*? Spelled a-e-b-l-e-s-k-i-v-e-r-s. I looked it up last night."

My uncle scoops four of them onto her plate and ladles blueberries over the top. "I like our word for it better."

She shrugs. "Yeah, well, I think it's better to have all the information first. Then when you screw with it, it's because you're nonconformist and not because you're ignorant."

Dad's pushing his *ebel-skeebers* back and forth with his fork. "It's not helping your health, not sleeping," he says. "It's going to be hard enough to get your vision and your hands back to normal, if they're *going* to get back to normal, when you're sleeping. I saw your computer this morning—there are like two new chapters there. Usually that takes you three days, at least. If you're not going to help yourself . . ." he grumbles. He stabs lackadaisically at the pile of *ebel-skeebers*, and one of them rolls off the edge of the plate. He leaves it there.

"Well, I'm sorry, Michael," Mom says. "There are apparently enough chemicals in my body to keep me running in schizo mode for the next two weeks. Once they work their way out, I'll slow down. I promise. Besides, I'm helping myself. I didn't *just* write last night. I researched alternative ways I could use to help manage the MS. Besides regular doctors and regular US medicine—you all know how I feel about those and that—I found lots of alternative treatments. I'm thinking about finding an acupuncturist. Or maybe a naturopath."

"And don't forget," I chime in, "We are now nonconformist about *ebel-skeebers*." *I kind of like that we both looked that up. I don't want to tell THEM I already looked it up, because that would seem, oh, I don't know, like I'm trying too hard to prove I'm not a troll, maybe. Just because my uncle's boyfriend is convinced I'm not a troll doesn't mean . . .* But I can't hide the little smile.

"Yes, bella," says Uncle Pasta. "Nonconformist about ze Danish round pancakes. Not-a-ignoramuses."

"Yes, well," Dad sulks. "I don't like it."

Mom reaches over to pat him on the arm. "I know, honey. I know you only feel protective and worried, and I know it's out of love and concern. I promise as soon as the steroids are gone, I will concentrate on sleeping." She turns her focus to me. "But now that I seem to have all this random energy, let's talk about Cora."

"OK," I say. "You know her uncle is out of the house. He has to stay at least five hundred feet away from her until the investigation is complete. Which means, hopefully, until they convict him, and then that ass hat has to stay at least five hundred feet away from her forever and ever and ever. I wish the law said five thousand feet. Heck, five million feet away, that would make me really happy."

"*Si, sí!*" says Uncle Pasta. "That should put him right into a nice studio apartment in Sri Lanka." He scoops a forkful of pastry, and rolls it around his mouth, apparently in ecstasy at the thought of Lucas Perkins in Sri Lanka. Or maybe it's the *ebel-skeeber*.

I chop mine in half with my fork. "No, no studio apartment. He needs a nice large cell in Sing Sing. With lots of roommates."

Mom claps her hands. "Oooh, yeah. We all know how other prisoners feel about child molesters. Molesters get shivved in prison. Such a great word, 'shivved.' Maybe the villain in my next book should get 'shivved.'"

Dad snorts and pushes his untouched plate away. "You guys rely on *way* too much of your quote-unquote education coming from TV and the movies." He stands. "Harper, I know this isn't really the appropriate thing to ask, but Cora has seen her father since Thursday, hasn't she?"

I nod.

"Did you tell her about the fight I had with him when you spoke to her on Thursday night?"

"I did, but she didn't even seem to hardly register it. That's when I also told her about Mom, and she was really upset about that. She kept saying 'multiple sclerosis? How can she have multiple sclerosis? That sounds worse than cancer.' And I told her it wasn't worse, not really, because it doesn't kill you. But hey Mom, the fact that you couldn't see was really freaking her out. I need to call her and tell her how well you're doing today."

I smile at Mom, and she beams across the table at me. She's looking right at me, too!

"Anyway, she told me her dad was really not talking to her when he came in on Thursday at dinnertime, and he just said, quietly but sarcastically, 'Well, your uncle is gone from the house, thanks to your friend and her mother.'" All of a sudden, I feel myself getting misty. "She was all matter of fact about it, like it didn't really matter to her that her dad was choosing that criminal over his daughter." *And here we are, making jokes about it.* I sniff. "I don't think he said anything to her about his bruised-up face or about Mom collapsing."

Uncle Pasta has an *ebel-skeeber* on the end of his fork, and he gestures it toward my Dad. "Michael, I bet he isn't going to say squat to the police." He pops it in his mouth, then speaks through a mouthful of mush, "I bet he feelsth resthponsible for Isabelle's collapsthe." He swallows. "He's probably afraid you'll send the police after *him* for causing Isabelle to collapse. Maybe he's even worried he hit her."

"Yeah," I nod toward Mom. "It was so crazy there for a while. You and Mr. Perkins were, like, nose to nose and everyone was shouting and then Dad shows up like the wrath of God.... I can see that. He's probably scared."

Dad interlaces his hands behind his neck and stands there, leaning his head back against them. He stares at the ceiling for a minute, then whooshes out a big breath. "That makes sense. You're probably right. I don't think he'll press any charges against me. You're probably right," he repeats.

That's right, Daddy, I think. *You stop worrying so much. Everything will be OK.*

"I'm going to go take a shower," he says, and relief shapes his shoulders. "Try not to shiv anyone." He disappears up the stairs.

Mom and Uncle eye each other across the table. "He tried

to make a little funny there," Mom says. "That's a good sign."

I shove the last *ebel-skeeber* in. "So, Mom, Uncle Pasta. What are we going to do today? Something relaxing for you, Mom."

"I don't care, as long as it's with you guys. Something I can look at, that sounds good. A movie?"

"Oooh!" says Uncle Pasta. "There's a classic movie marathon at the Avalon."

"We could go to the botanical gardens," I say. "There's a butterfly house, you know."

Mom splays both hands out, weighing the options. "I choose . . . both."

Yay, both! We all grab hands around the table, again the Cleavers in a campy, cheesy show of love and solidarity, and for a minute I forget about MS and Cora and Larson, and just revel in our ability to see each other and our plan to go see things together.

24. PrEMaTuRe

premature /premə'CHoor/ adj. occurring or done before the usual or proper time; too early.

✪✪✪

We actually only got to see part of one movie, and no butterfly house. Mom's hands stopped working altogether and couldn't even grab the popcorn, and Dad called Dr. Ammon right away. The doctor explained that she was still in the middle of the stress-related aggravation of her MS symptoms, and that her brain was still inflamed, and that she needed to be taking it *very easy*.

Dad helped her down Main Street, lecturing, "*Very easy* does not mean carousing around town with a plan that would wear out someone at the peak of health, much less someone who is . . . inflamed, and has a scar on her brain."

Uncle Pasta and I trailed behind them, feeling horrible and guilty and worried all over again.

When we get home, we all hover. Dad makes her stay in bed, and we bring her food and her books to her—but not the computer, because we know it'll be hard to type anything, and that will just frustrate her. The fork frustrates her enough. She calls us a "helicopter family" and tells us all to go away.

So for the rest of the weekedn we tiptoe around the house and try not to hover. Uncle Pasta locks himself in his downstairs apartment; Dad wanders around organizing things—the pantry, the silverware drawers, the hall closet—and I sit in my room and look things up.

I find out "multiple sclerosis" means "many scars." I read testimonials from people claiming things like bee venom and peanut butter had cured their MS. I also look up laws in the state of Colorado concerning child molesters. There are levels of molestation, apparently, like levels of murder, and Lucas Perkins has committed the worst type—obviously. *Sicko.* He was "an adult in a position of trust and power," and those convictions can bring a sentence of twenty years to life in prison. *Yeah, Uncle Lucas, you can rot.*

I text Cora at the hospital, and she writes that someone from Social Services had been to see her yesterday, and had talked to her about her testimony. "Im scared, chkadee," the screen says.

I don't know what to text back. God, I couldn't imagine having to look that man in the eye after he had done something like that to me, and having to give details with him and a lot of strangers staring my way. Judging. In my mind, I see the man I had seen in the hospital lobby, and unwanted, horrific thoughts of his hands on my eight-year-old body make me gag. It's so sickening. I try to smack the thoughts out of my head, and I'm already afraid they'll haunt me forever.

What can I say to make her feel better? Her uncle's hands had been all over her for three years: He had raped her. Violated her. But worse, I think, she had *trusted* him. Trusted him and loved him, and he took her trust and slaughtered it. I don't know how she can ever recover.

I stare at the cell phone screen again. "*I'm scared.*"

Oh, I am useless, so useless. Nothing even has to come out of my mouth, because here is the perfect opportunity to write something comforting, I can contemplate it and write the perfect words to make her feel better, make her feel like we can combine some as-yet-untapped superhero powers and banish Lucas Perkins straight to hell with our mystical mojo. What is wrong with me? My fingers freeze on the keypad like they're glued there.

I close my eyes and think about my mother. She is so brave and she *is* my mother. I know she is, and she uses her words and her heart to make people feel better all the time.

I drop the cell phone and pick up my prehistoric house phone to dial the hospital. "Cora? It's me. I know you're scared. I also know you're strong. You're strong, and solid, and you can do this. You can face your uncle, and even if your dad's not there for you, *my* dad will be there for you. And my mom. You are like family to them. And then there's me. You're my best friend, Cora, and I don't think you have any idea how much your kind nature and good humor mean to me, and keep me going when I feel like I'm useless and unfunny and not being helpful or interesting to *anyone*. I know you can do this. You can make your uncle answer for what he did, and then maybe, just maybe, you can start to heal. I'll be there for you, and when you need someone, in the courtroom, or any old time, ever, you can look right at me, and you can draw strength from me. I love you to pieces, and you can draw strength from me."

I stop to breathe. *That wasn't so bad, for not being rehearsed. I don't think.* I don't hear anything on the other end. "Cora?"

I hear a deep, shuddering breath. A sob. "I love you to pieces, too, chickadee," she hiccups. "Thank you. I needed to hear you say that." I listen to her crying on the other end, and I don't say anything else. She breathes heavily another couple of times, with an "unh, unh." I can hear her tears winding down like a clock. Then, a heart-wrenching sigh. "The woman from Social Services said someone would be in to talk to me tomorrow, and that she thought there would be an arraignment on Tuesday. I don't know if I need to be there for that or not, but I think maybe I should be there for everything."

"I'll be there with you."

"Don't you need to be home with Isabelle?"

"Ooh, Isabelle can see again, sort of. Did I tell you that? But her hands aren't working and the doctor told her she had to stay home and take it very easy, so we were trying to take care of her, but she told us we were hovering like a helicopter family and banished us to other parts of the house. I've been in my room all day looking things up, and I guess Uncle Pasta is working downstairs at his place. I don't know where my dad is right at this moment, but it wouldn't surprise me if he was just perched outside of their bedroom, out of sight but ready to spring like a cat if he hears any noises that sound like distress signals."

"He's kind of intense like that, isn't he?" muses Cora, and I can hear her relief at the change of topic.

"Well, yeah. I didn't totally get *how* intense until Mom got sick."

"Now, tell me again what your uncle does for a living? It seems like he's home whenever he wants to be."

"He writes things."

"Just . . . things? Books like your mom?"

I leap with both feet onto the change-of-topic train. "No, I guess he's a cross between my mom and my dad, interestingly enough. I mean, I don't know how my dad feels about the comparison, but . . . he writes all sorts of things, jingles for radio or TV commercials, children's songs, whatever he's obsessing about at that particular moment. He used to be a medical transcriptionist, but he said that kind of writing gave him narcolepsy. Don't ask me how he started making money at his kinds of writing, or how he first got published, because this all happened when I was like five years old. To this day I'm not sure how he does it."

"Maybe the jingle thing is just a cover for his CIA job."

"Yeah, I'm sure the terrorists would spill their secrets immediately when he pulled out a gun with two fingers and his pinky cocked like he's at a tea party."

She laughs, and boy, does *that* sound nice. "That would make me start talking, for sure. And if that didn't do it, his spaghetti trick would."

I giggle with her. "I still don't understand how he keeps the spaghetti from breaking when it's in his nose or throat."

We laugh together, longer than the situation calls for, I'm sure.

"Hey," she says. "What do you call a defective boomerang?"

"I don't know."

"A stick."

"OK, OK," I say. "I've got one for you. What do you get when you cross an alligator and a railroad track?"

Gales of laughter explode through the phone. "Three pieces of alligator! I love that one. Say, speaking of pieces of amphibians, what's up with luscious Larson and cat dissection?"

"Cats aren't amphibians."

"No, I know, but frogs are, and that's another thing you dissect. It's the only way I could make a good transition to ask you about Larson."

"Oh, and gee, you certainly are the sovereign of the segue, aren't you? I saw Larson earlier in the week. I hardly remember it, there was so much other stuff going on."

"Oh, baloney. The sky could literally be falling and you'd still remember every word he said as the clouds busted open around your heads." I can hear the grin in her voice.

"OK, Ohh-kay! We took a tour through Spike's digestive system, and he did give me a smile to die for as he called me over to our table. Larson did, not Spike."

"So, you are going to see him tomorrow, right? Was that the last stop on the kitty tour?"

"I think so. But I'm sure there's more to do—cleanups, writeups . . ."

"Loveups?" I swear, I can *hear* her arching her eyebrows up and down like Groucho Marx, and I lounge in a too-brief feeling that all the nastiness hasn't happened, and we're just screwing around, like normal.

"Oh. My. God. You are such a goon. Yes, I guess I'm going to school, if you don't have any court stuff. My parents are so adamant about taking advantage of our free public education. Plus, I'm banished from taking care of Mom, right? Queen of the Amazons." Something occurs to me. "How much longer are you going to be in the hospital?" *How is she going to deal with her dad?* "Isn't it going to be hard for you . . . going home?"

A small pause. "No, I don't think so. My dad may be mad at me for telling on Uncle Lucas, but it's not like he scares me. He may not speak to me much when we get home, but it's not like we had long father-daughter walks in the park before . . . before all this. I think it'll be OK."

"Are you sure?"

"I'm sure. Go to school, chickadee. Have a loveup with Larson."

I snort. "Or at the very least, I can continue vicariously participating in his ongoing loveup with Spike. So, bye. Sleep tight."

"Bye." I hang up my decrepit phone. *Well, then. I think she might be OK.*

25. iNTRoDuCTioN

introduction /ˈintrə dəkSH(ə)n/ n. the action of introducing something.

ʘʘʘ

Monday's walk to school felt, for some reason, like the first day of high school all over again—I was kind of nervous.

The elderly man is bringing up the rear of the *tai chi* foursome, and I'm inordinately glad to see them all together. I salute the group as they inch by. There's no hitch to their ultra-slow and smooth movements, but the man in the rear winks at me, I'm pretty sure.

The September weather has entered into that all-too-brief season in Colorado known as fall—everybody's favorite around here. We wish it here and then wish it back when it's gone, like our best dream. The leaves on the row of trees lining the center of my street have slowly mellowed, in their own way, toward yellows and reds which'll soon paint the road in a rustling rainbow of earth tones that can't help but make people happy.

I reach the end of my street, make a left on the next street and then another left and soon arrive at the front of Pinewood

High School. It stretches along two blocks of, logically, Pine Street, and because it's so long, it looks like a college campus with a few students milling around or sitting under the trees in the courtyard. *Only* a few students, because it's just 6:45, and the torrent won't start until like five minutes before the 7:30 bell.

Cade Castell is one of the early birds crazy enough to get here before he actually has to be. He lounges, cross-legged, against a giant elm tree outside the auditorium. Mentally preparing for acting class? I don't know. He could be people watching, but the whole lack of people makes me wonder.

"Hey," he says to me. "Want to be my partner for the I-don't-know-you-but-I-might-want-to-play-a-character-like-you-on-stage-someday game?" He reaches up to touch at his eyebrow ring, looking at me expectantly.

I'd really like to know if it hurt to poke all those holes in your face, I think, but instead I say, "Huh?"

He drops his hands to his knees and leans forward. "Don't you remember? When the sub read Miss Bakener's plans for this week, he said, in that don't-look-now-but-I'm-already-dead voice of his, that we were going to do a get-to-know-someone-we-don't sort of game on Monday, and we're supposed to be finding someone we don't spend a lot of time with to be our partner. I'm not surprised you missed it; he didn't exactly have a stellar stage presence."

"Oh, you mean the Crypt Keeper? No, I guess I wasn't really tuned in to my education on Friday."

"I know . . . that guy was a *dead* ringer." He slaps his knee and gives a "yuk yuk yuk" laugh straight out of a mausoleum, it's that creepy. But he seems so jolly and proud of himself for making the joke, I have to giggle. "I have those old *Tales from the Crypt* episodes on Blu-ray," he says. "What's your favorite episode?"

I can feel the heat of a blush. "Well, I'm ashamed to admit it. But I can't help but remember the one with a young Brad Pitt. You?"

"I like the one about the overzealous dude who ends up in pieces in all those neat-freakishly labeled, well-organized jars," he says. "I don't know, I just dig anything with such a finely tuned sense of karma, even if it uses blood and gore to make the point, ya know?"

"I know, right? I hate it when bad people don't get what's coming to them, and when good people . . ." My voice trails off. "It's just too bad the world doesn't really work that way." I don't really want to go there, so I say, "Tell me more about your favorite *Crypt* episodes. That'll help me get to know you."

He complies, and we talk for ten minutes about the karmic appropriateness of the horror show. But Cade's a little nosy, apparently, and I can't keep him off topic forever.

"Hey, are you OK? You looked pretty freaked when I handed you that worksheet on Friday. I didn't want to pry. Someone not getting the dose of cosmic justice they deserve?"

I shrug. "Just . . . lots of stuff going on."

The first bell rings, and I look up to notice the usual last-minute influx of students flooding the campus. I hadn't even felt their numbers building.

"Maybe I'll tell you about it in the get-to-know-me game. In case you want to give yourself a perm and play 'Harper' on stage some time."

He flips his shiny smooth black ponytail and grins, then helps me up from the oak tree to lead me straight into the hormone tsunami otherwise known as high school.

PE and Algebra do nothing to educate, enlighten, or even amuse me, because I spend both classes remembering the smile I'd gotten from Larson last week and working myself into a tizzy, as other teenagers say *not ever*, over what might happen in Anatomy today.

What if he asks me out? I think I should start a conversation about his interests, and maybe he'll find something we're both interested in and suggest we do that thing together. Or maybe I could find something that interests us both and suggest we do it together.

Or maybe Mr. Wolfram will drop to one khakied knee and suggest that he and I run away together and make beautiful babies whom we'll dress in Hawaiian-print onesies, because that's about how likely it is I'll have the guts to ask Larson to do anything. Even if we get to spend the whole period discussing the merits of my favorite book, which he just HAPPENED to finish over the weekend, I still strenuously doubt my level of courage on this matter.

The only time I get distracted from my tizzy is when a girl named Amber brushes by me on the football field. I get that same knee-twitch I had before Cora cut her wrists. I watch Amber on the obstacle course, but even when she falls into one of the tires, she comes up laughing and she doesn't look depressed or maudlin. *Shows what I know.* These signs don't tell me anything. Might as well have a sign on *my* forehead saying "I have useless twitching body parts. Ask me how!" Hmph.

At the bell, I try motoring through the halls like a speed walker because I want to get to Anatomy before Larson. I don't know why I came up with this speed walking plan.

I've never really noticed it before, I guess, but this school is chock *full* of people. And they apparently like to congregate in large groups between classes, groups that stretch from one side of the hall to the other, practically, except for one teensy little space travelers can sneak their way through, single file. By the time I've thrust my way through about five of these groups,

I'm more flustered than before and looking the part, I'm sure.

And Larson is already there.

How does he get through that nightmare hallway and come out the other side untouched? And looking SO fine. Damnit. I try smoothing my hair, and stop smoothing at my ear because he looks up with that gorgeous, slightly crooked dimpled grin. I'm caught. Reel me in with poofy hair, deposit me on the beach, and fry me up, because I'm hooked by that smile.

"Hey, Harper," he says. Spike is laid out on our table already, and Larson has the scalpel poised. "Are you feeling better today? Is your friend Cora doing OK?"

How does he know about Cora? "How do you know about my friend Cora, just out of curiosity?"

"Everybody knows about your friend Cora. The whole school's talking about it—hot mysterious chick tries to slit her wrists." He uses the scalpel to pantomime the motion. "As my friend Mike says—he's totally in love with her, by the way—it makes her even more hot and mysterious. Anyway, you scrammed out of here so fast on Friday. I didn't mean to bum you out. Is she going to be OK?"

I'm looking at the scalpel, a little horrified by his casual movement. "Yes, she's . . ."

Mr. Wolfram interrupts, which is a good thing because I'm just about to tell Larson something I shouldn't about why Cora was so mysterious, just to get him to focus on me a little bit longer. "Class, I'm afraid today is the last official day we get to explore a new organ in our cats . . . then it's all cleanups and writeups."

Loveups?

"So get your scalpels and your probes out. We are going to delve into . . ." He pauses for dramatic effect. "Da da da DAHHHH! The cardiovascular system! First, you must remove the pericardial sac and then you get to cut up and explore the chambers of the heart and its lovely little valves, the chordae tendinae, the aorta, the superior and inferior vena cava, the pulmonary artery, and—for extra credit—see if you can identify the coronary blood vessels. Go ahead and pull out your tools, and I'll walk around and help anyone who needs it. Also, don't forget to check the projector screen for the diagrams to use for help in knowing where to cut."

Before Mr. Wolfram has even finished talking, he walks toward two girls who look clueless and frustrated.

Larson hands me a scalpel. "Do you want to start, or should I? You look like the heartbreaker out of both of us, so maybe you should start."

"I . . . I look like the heartbreaker?" I'm stammering before he even finishes his sentence. *Oh. My. God. I think he's flirting. Say something. Flirt back. Go.* "No, it has to be you, with all the . . . basketball fame and all." *Brilliant.*

He snorts. "Yeah, sure thing, you would know about my fame. You didn't even know when my season starts."

Of course he remembers THAT with crystal clarity.

He guides the scalpel around the covering of Spike's heart, and I try to pull it free. *Eeuw.* "Dude, I'm for sure not gonna get famous playing basketball. Gimme a break."

"So, Larson." *Lllllarson.* "What *are* you going to get famous for? Are you going to write the 'Great American Novel'? Win a Nobel Peace Prize for curing cancer?" I say. *Either one would be fantastic. And see, that was an OK response. Conversation is happening. It's growing. We're heading toward sixty-odd years together, moving slowly and in perfect harmony.*

"Naw," he says. "I don't even like reading much. And the cancer thing would be cool, and all, but . . ." he takes the scalpel and slams it into of the middle of the sac I'd been working on so carefully, and it just sort of falls off.

Eeuw.

"Naw, I was thinking football. I think I'll be the next John

Elway, except he went to Stanford and they'll have to draft me out of a much cheaper school, 'cuz there's no way I'm gonna get into Stanford. Plus, he's a quarterback, and I'm a running back. But he's like, the most famous player that comes to mind, and I thought, well, Harper's heard of him for sure, so she can like . . . relate." He places his hand on top of mine. "You do know who John Elway is, right?"

He guides my hand over to this little tough section of Spike's teeny heart, and I assume this is one of the chambers we're supposed to be exploring. *Oh, crap, why couldn't I have paid attention just one time when Dad watched his sports? This beautiful boy is kinda, almost, holding my hand right now and I don't know a football from a submarine sandwich.* "Ah, sure I know. He's a . . . famous quarterback. A . . . famous Californian quarterback?"

"He just went to California in college, goofball. He's a Denver Bronco, so, a Colorado player. That's why I figured you'd know. Well, he used to be a Denver Bronco. He's retired now, but man, he's a famous Denver Bronco—the first Bronco to be inducted into the Pro Football Hall of Fame. He's *hall-of-fame* famous, baby. How can you not know that?"

Larson pulls the section of the heart free that I had been cutting and peers into it. "I'm not sure what we're supposed to be studying in this heart cavity. Looks kinda like mush to me." He steps back and surveys Spike's remains, which all look a little bit mushy to me.

And then there's the smell, which I had somehow gotten used to, but when I consider it, really stays perched on my way-interior nose hairs, vibrating there. "No," I say. "I guess I don't really know that much about it."

He starts trying to display the cuttings we have made, because Mr. Wolfram is doing rounds to check on our progress. "Know that much about what?" he murmurs.

"Football. Famous football players. John Elway."

"Oh, right. Well, no biggie. There's lots of other, newer famous ones. I could teach you about some of them, if you want."

I really couldn't care less about football players of any kind but, still . . . *he can teach me anything he wants.* I try again. "So, Larson. Your last name's McCready, right?" He nods. "That's Irish, right?"

He stops pushing parts to look at me. "I dunno," he shrugs, "I guess."

Doesn't everybody know their ethnic background? "Because . . . because I was just going to say, I'm part Irish. My mother's maiden name is O'Dwyer. So see, we have something in common —we're both at least partway from the land o' the leprechauns!" *And one of us is at least partway losing her mind here. Help me out pleeeese, would ya, hot leprechaun?*

"Hmph. I dunno," he says. "I don't really think it's all that important to know where my, like, ancestors were born or whatever. What matters is that we are all American!" He picks up what's left of Spike's arms and claps them together, as if Spike is applauding his patriotism.

"Hmmm. Of course, that's crucial. Us being Americans. I don't know what I was doing, thinking where we came from might be important in figuring out where we're going." I show my glove-encased palms to the sky. "Call me crazy."

"Yep, you are one crazy chick, Harper."

He gives me the grin again, and I feel like I'm going to cry, he's so aggravatingly cute. I have to stay on this train, although it seems to be hurtling directly into the side of a big mountain.

"So, what are some of your other favorite things to do, Larson McCready, possibly-Irish-but-certainly-American?" *Would you like to ride horses in the moonlight? Serenade me by candlelight in Circle Park? Ponder our karmic reason for existing on this planet, while kissing?*

"Man, that's tough. Lemme think." He strokes his chin to

give me the visual. "I don't really like baseball. Too slow. Mike and me were thinking about starting a water polo team here, except we just have that dinky community pool. We need *Olympic size*, baby. I don't know, soccer's OK, I guess, although Mike keeps telling me to get off of *that* plan, 'cuz he thinks soccer's for pussies."

He tosses his scalpel onto the table. "I'm getting a little tired of this cat thing. Let's just write it up and move on, huh?" He turns to Mr. Wolfram, who's almost to us, anyway. "Hey, Wolfie. What are we doing next in this class? Spike's starting to get boring."

Mr. Wolfram pats Larson on the shoulder. "Well, then, you'll be happy to know, m'boy, that after we're finished with the writeups on cat dissection, we're going to start studying a much bigger specimen: the human body. Maybe you and Harper can be partners again when we get to the section on the most powerful organ . . ."

Larson bursts out laughing. "Hey Wolfie, you're hilarious! Prolly shouldn't be talkin' about that stuff in front of Harper, though."

Mr. Wolfram has a twinkle in his eye. "Harper already knows a lot about the power of this organ, because hers works so well, and I am, naturally, talking about the brain, Larson. The human brain, the most amazing tool we have." He winks at me, and of course, here come the hives.

I just can't win.

Larson has moved on to cleanup and isn't paying all that much attention, anyway, which gives the redness a chance to recede. I thought I would make one more desperate attempt. "Is there anything you like to do for fun besides sports, Larson?"

He starts packing up our tools. "Hmmm. Let me see. Yeah, fishing. I really like to fish—my dad got me into it last year. I even like deboning them and cleaning out the guts, because then they taste so sick on a skillet around the campfire." He gives me the smile, and it's still gorgeous. I guess.

I can't stop the sigh. "Yeah. I've heard that's fun, too."

Reel me in, Larson. Reel me in.

26. aPPreHeNSioN

apprehension /aprə'henSHən/ n. anxiety or fear that something bad or unpleasant will happen.

⟲⟲⟲

The kitchen table is chock full of Southwoods and O'Dwyers this morning, because Cora called last night to tell me there's going to be something going on today with her uncle, maybe at the courthouse.

I was thinking about the debacle yesterday otherwise known as cat dissection with Larson All-American-doesn't-read-books-or-care-about-anything-but-sports McCready. *I can't believe people just don't have any stake in where they come from. I—if I am indeed a genetic O'Dwyer slash Southwood instead of a subterranean earth dweller—care about where I come from and where I'm going. Not to the football field and not to the lake, that's where.*

My brain rambles on, because I don't want to think about Larson any more. *I don't have the slightest idea why Uncle Pasta, Peter O'Dwyer, affects the Italian accent. Maybe because an Irish accent is too hard and not as fun.* Anyway, I guess O'Dwyers are what's known as "Black Irish" because they have dark hair and eyes. Oh, I guess that's what I'd be known as, too, although Dad is all German. So I'm German Black Irish.

That is, provided I really am a genetic part of this family, which I'm starting to think . . . maybe I am. Maybe. Of course, there're still all those body parts of mine that seem to wig out of their own accord, but that's not really a troll quality, anyway—at least not one I've been able to find. Are my whacked-out bodily tendencies of experiencing impending illness through tingles, twitches, stabs of pain, or other unexpected manifestations a *quality*, even? The word makes it sound useful, and I'm pretty sure it is not in the slightest.

I walk down the stairs and take in the scene in the kitchen. Mom's sitting at the table trying to work her fingers, that exercise where you click each finger to the thumb: one, two, three, four, and then back. Her black hair is a crush of curls knotted together to perch in a nest on top of her head, and the nest jiggles while she works.

She does it snap-diddly-snap with her left hand, but on the right her forefinger and fourth finger keep missing the thumb, and I can see she's getting mad.

"Well, shit," she says. "I guess it's a good thing I'm left handed." She shakes both hands out and addresses me. "So, Harper, what did Cora say? Are we taking you to the courthouse, or what?"

"No, I told her we'd pick her up at the hospital. I'm bringing her some of my clothes instead of going to get hers, because I'm scared of Mr. Perkins. Then, I guess we're starting back at the RMCFC, meeting with Officer Lenox. He told her he met with the district attorney yesterday, and they definitely want to press charges. Lucas Perkins hasn't been arrested yet, though, which sucks, don't you think?" I cross the kitchen floor and open the pantry, craving some Oatmeal Squares.

Uncle Pasta is sitting opposite from Mom, finishing a bowl of fruit. He reaches across the maroon tablecloth to start rubbing her fingers. "That does suck, bella. Why hasn't he been arrested yet? Aren't they afraid he'll retaliate against Cora for snitching on him?"

"I am afraid of that." Pouring the cereal and some milk into a bowl and setting it down next to Mom, I grab her other hand so I can rub her fingers, too. "Cora doesn't seem to be. She says his big muscles are all a front and he's not really *physically* frightening. She's scared to testify in court about what happened to her, because holy cow, that seems like it would be so hard, but she doesn't seem to think he's a threat otherwise. I guess Officer Lenox agrees, and he told her it was standard in child molestation cases that they don't arrest the guy until they feel they've accumulated a strong enough case."

Mom throws up her weakened hands. "Well, I'm sure you all know how I feel about *that*."

"Hmmm," I say. "You think that's bullshit? Sorry, Dad, I know, 'don't be crude.'"

He's standing in the doorway knotting his tie. "No, Harper, at this point I have to agree. It is bullshit. Isabelle, why don't I just call in sick? I can drive the girls. You should be resting. You know what the doctor said. He said—"

"Yeah, yeah, I know. He said take it easy. I could possibly ease myself into a psychotic meltdown if I have to stay here and tear out my hair while my daughter and her best friend deal with this aforementioned bullshit."

"I can drive them," says Uncle Pasta. "Isabelle will sit demurely in the front seat taking it easy, Harper and Cora will sit in the back prepping for the incarceration of Lucas Perkins, and no one will do anything remotely psychotic or melty."

"Yeah, Dad. Go ahead and go to work." I squeeze Mom's fingers one last time, and set her hand down gently on the table.

"I mean, what if we see Lucas there? Or Joseph? Neither one of them are scary, really, but *you* sure were last time you saw one of them." I shove a bunch of Oatmeal Squares into my mouth, eager to start the day.

Uncle Pasta swishes his hand. "You sure were thcary. You're thuch a manly thtud."

Dad, of course, shakes his head and goes back upstairs.

"Peter," Mom pokes him on the shoulder, "why do you torture that poor man? I think he's doing pretty well with the whole homophobia thing, considering."

"I know, I know, I'm sorry," he says. "He does great. I know it's hard. I guess I keep thinking immersion in the stereotype might tweak his sense-of-humor button and help him relax." He kisses Mom's fingertips.

"Considering?" I ask, spooning in a giant bite of squares and chewing while I talk, which Dad hates, but hey, he's back upstairs. "Considering what? How come there're all these stories I don't know? Uncle Pasta, I really don't know how you got started writing jingles, or even if that's what you really do, and I don't know why Dad is so uncomfortable around gay men."

"Hmm. You're suspicious about my secret CIA job, maybe?"

Mom continues the finger exercise, just with her right hand now. "You didn't really know your grandparents, Harper, since they both died before you were born. Your dad grew up in a very conservative family. You know, homosexuality is a sin against God, blah blah blah. He didn't really believe that once he got to adulthood, but then he had this college roommate who was gay."

"So, what?" I ask. I can hear Dad slamming drawers upstairs.

"Soooo," says Uncle Pasta. "This roommate was also a teammate on your dad's baseball team. So the roommate wasn't *telling* anyone he was gay, of course. He just went around making fag jokes with the others. But . . ."

"But he really had fallen for your dad," says Mom. "One

night, he crawled in bed with Dad and started kissing the back of his neck, professing his undying love."

I gasp, and my hand pops over my mouth. "Ohmigosh. I bet Dad freaked. Did he hit the guy?"

"Peter, those squares look good. Will you get me some?" Mom's eyeing my breakfast. "No, he just jumped out of bed, I guess. Told the roommate he didn't feel that way, and went over to another friend's apartment. Moved out the next week, never told his teammates why. I guess he was really good friends with this guy, and the whole situation just . . . scarred him."

"But that's just one guy," I say. "One scared, lonely teenage guy. What does he have to do with gay people in general?" Although when I think about it, should I blame my dad for his reaction to feeling violated?

"Nothing," Mom replies, blowing a kiss to Uncle Pasta when he sets a bowl of squares in front of her. "Absolutely nothing, but you don't know what a mature point of view that is, sweetheart. That's why we're telling you all these stories now, because you have this fabulous outlook. Your dad knows the one doesn't relate to the other, either, it's just . . ."

"It's just that he looks at me or at Charles," says my uncle, "and he can't help but remember that kiss on the neck, and all the nonsense he heard from his parents for so many years. It freaks him out a little. He can't help it, he's human, and I shouldn't give him such a hard time." He sighs.

Mom smacks him on the shoulder. "Come on. Cora's waiting."

I jump up. "Yeah, let's go get her. By the way, Cora is the one who suspects the secret CIA job."

"Well, she's not as smart as she thinks she is," he grins. "It's NSA, not CIA. *Much* more secretive and subversive. Fewer rules and better weapons."

We each grab Mom by a hand and lead her on our mission.

※※※

Cora and I sit in the back of the Honda, and I fill her in on my dad's college roommate, just to tell stories and get her mind off where we're going. Cora has never been to the Rocky Mountain Center for Children: Officer Lenox videotaped her interview from her hospital bed.

She'd met Louisa Tripoli in the hospital, too—she's Cora's advocate. But Cora doesn't know Louisa's story, so I fill her in. I don't know for sure, but I think the story about my dad and the roommate who loved him surprised her and the story about Louisa made her feel stronger, more ready somehow to face what she has to face. *I hope so.*

It's a really nice day outside, and the RMCFC still looks like an anonymous building but today somehow it's more welcoming. I grab her hand as we walk in and squeeze.

"Hmmm," she says. "Looks sort of like a daycare."

I leave her to look around, and head back to the car so Uncle Pasta and I can help Mom. Mom allows us to hold her, each of us taking one arm, but her hesitating steps about break my heart.

"Louisa! Tom!" she calls, and her boisterous voice belies her faltering walk. "I've got notes for characters based on BOTH of you in my next book. You're going to be famous! Under alternate names to protect your identities, of course. So, secretly famous."

Officer Lenox and Louisa help take her by each elbow to lead her to the couch in the meeting room. Neither one says a word or asks about her difficulty walking. *I guess their discretion carries over into all parts of life. Good to know.*

"Hi there, Harper, Cora, and Isabelle," says Officer Lenox. "We're so glad you're here."

Mom and Uncle Pasta sit on the couch, but Louisa leads me

and Cora to a square table surrounded by four padded office chairs.

"Tom's been working hard on the case, Cora," says Louisa, "and we should be ready to arrest your uncle sometime this week. Tom even spent the weekend working on it—talked to your dad and everything."

"And what did my dad say?" Cora wonders. "He's not really speaking to me right now." She flips her hands upward on the table, and studies the white bandages on her wrists. They're much smaller than the wraps she had at the hospital.

"No, I know. I get it," Officer Lenox says. "He just can't believe his brother would do something like that. And when your mom was sick."

Cora's bottom lip quavers. "He can't believe my uncle would . . . but he believes *I would make up* a horrible story like that? Just to hurt him?" She looks over at me, eyes swimming. *How can anyone be so awful? I don't understand . . .* say her eyes.

I try to answer her with mine. *You are strong and solid. We are all there for you. You can do this.*

"I know, that must be hurtful," says Officer Tom.

Louisa, sitting next to Cora, squeezes her shoulder.

"I think he does believe you, really, Cora," Tom says. "He just doesn't know how to admit it. It's just . . ."

"If he has to admit what was going on in his house and he didn't see it . . ." interrupts Louisa. "If he says he believes you, that means he failed you. And he already thinks he failed you because he couldn't save your mom. I guarantee it."

Louisa's comments make a perfect kind of sick, sad sense to me. I've been feeling like I failed my mom because I couldn't tell she was getting sick, even with the evidence of her symptoms right in front of me. Mr. Perkins must have been so twisted up with concern over his wife's cancer, and so happy for any kind of help from his brother—the brother he loved so much. I could see how he might have missed the signs.

Cora's face settles into a kind of resignation. "I guess I can see that. But my uncle must have known what he did to me was wrong. And I want to make him pay for it, and like totally make sure he never does it to anyone else, with or without my father's help. Do I have to talk about everything he did in court? In front of him and everyone? Do I have to talk about *everything*?" A shadow of fear ripples Cora's steely resolve, and I remember the brief flash I'd had of her uncle with his hands on my childlike body.

That was just a flash, mind you. I can't imagine having to live through three years of that hell, and then having to verbally and emotionally relive it in front of people years later. *No one should have to do that.*

Officer Tom and Louisa exchange glances, and I know they're thinking the same thing, and have seen the same thing, before.

"Yes, Cora," the officer says. "If it gets to trial, you'll have to tell it all. And that Lucas is meaner'n a wet panther, so his lawyer will make you describe it in graphic detail, probably more than once, to try and see if your story changes." He shakes his head. His accent deepens with sympathy. "It's not pretty, ma'am. It's goin' to get worse before it gets better. Unless . . ."

Mom, Uncle Pasta, and I jump in all at once. "Unless what?"

And then I say, "What do you mean, *if* it gets to trial? I thought you said the DA wants to press charges for sure."

Louisa nods. "He did. He does. It's going to go to trial, unless we can get Lucas Perkins to plead out. To plead guilty to the charges."

"Ha!" scoffs Cora. "There's no way, not with him and my dad both denying the story."

"Well." Officer Tom continues, "There's another possibility. Something that would avoid trial. It's called a pretext call. I don't know if it would work in this case, though."

"What is it?" I demand, "and why won't it work in this case?" *Here's something interesting. A "pretext"—like a pretend way to get him. Maybe there's a way to get Lucas Perkins without making Cora cut her own heart out and plop it on the courtroom floor.*

Louisa holds Cora's hand. "A pretext call is just what it sounds like. If the molester is a family member, one of the other family members calls him on a pretext—to ask him a question or to get him to talk about the molestation. It's rehearsed and practiced ahead of time. Often the caller can get the molester to slip and say something incriminating about what he's done."

"The call is recorded, of course," confirms Officer Lenox. "Once we play the molester and his lawyer the recording, the lawyer almost always advises the molester to plead guilty to the charges, and then a trial is avoided."

Louisa straightens her shoulders and leans back in her chair. "The problem," she says, "is who, in your case, we can get to make the call. Because it can be very difficult for the victim to confront her molester, we usually try to get another family member to try. Things don't go as planned very often. It can be tricky to get him to say anything incriminating. Ideally, we would ask your father or mother to make the call."

Cora's face falls. "Obviously, my father's not going to do it. And my mother . . ." She grasps one of the bandages around her wrist.

God, she has to lose her mother all over again because of this asshole. She should never have to relive those years in any way, shape, or form.

"Does a family member have to make the call?" I ask. "Couldn't it be anyone who creates the pretext and gets him to talk?" I take a deep breath, because my brain's going crazy, thoughts pinging around in my skull like pinballs on steroids. *This is it. This is useful.* "Can I do it?"

Everyone in the room starts objecting at once.

"I can do it," says Mom. "He never even heard of Peter, and if Michael does it, he'll have his dander up right away because of what happened to Joseph."

No! I can do it. "Mom, you're sick," I say. "Nowhere in anyone's definition would confronting a child molester be considered 'taking it easy.'" I look from Cora to Louisa to Officer Tom Lenox, and over to my family, whom I am not always sure I deserve, but I see this as a chance to prove that I do. "I want to do it. I want to be the one who makes him pay." *Please.* I let my gaze travel around from Cora to Mom and back to the two nice people advocating for Cora.

Uncle Pasta looks at Mom and holds her hand tightly. She looks like her face is ready to explode with tears, and she's shaking her head no no no. I don't want to cause her more stress, but . . .

"Please?"

Uncle Pasta grabs both of Mom's hands. "Isabelle, I think you should let Harper help her friend, and we can all help her get through the pretext call."

She lets a huge breath go, and slowly nods her head.

Oh, God. "I think I can do it, Officer Tom. I can help Cora."

Officer Lenox, or "good ol' boy Tom" as I'm starting to see him, nods thoughtfully, and again, if he were wearing a hat, I'm sure he would tip it my way. "Harper, I think this is a right-good time for you to try."

27. UseFuLNeSS

usefulness /ˈyoosfəlnəs/ n. the quality or fact of being useful.

ᘛ ᘛ ᘛ

"Chickadee, are you sure?" Cora's face has tightened with alarm.

I breathe deeply, because the oxygen in this place has just plummeted to an intolerable level. *I'm sure of one thing: I don't have super powers. I'm sure I've gone my whole life without doing anything that's useful to anyone, including myself. I'm absolutely, utterly sure I need to start now, or it's not going to matter whether I'm troll, human, or amoeba.* "I'm sure. I want to help you, and if this means you don't have to tell your story in court, I will absolutely do my best to get your uncle to slip up."

Good ol' boy Tom looks over at my mom and my uncle, who both just stare at me. The room is silent, and they all stare. The clock goes tick-tick-tick, and no one speaks.

Finally, Mom breaks the silence. "Tom, is this normal, the friend confronting the abuser?"

"I don't think these situations are at all 'normal,'" he sighs. "The courts'll use whatever legal evidence is at their disposal to resolve the case, and if y'all are willing to let Harper try, I think she should be given the chance. Worst case scenario is it doesn't work, and then, Cora, we'll have to go to trial."

Mom looks at me again, searchingly. I watch her as she takes in my pleading expression, and then she gazes across the room at Cora hunched in an office chair. I watch Uncle Pasta squeeze her shoulder. She closes her eyes and takes a deep breath.

Then it's like she molts right in front of us. She sheds the worried aura that's been clinging to her skin like humid air, and smiles with all her teeth, and her eyes, too. She claps her hands once. "Well, then, I'm glad my beeyouteeful, smart little girl is going to help her friend. What does she need to do to prepare?"

Cora jumps off the chair to give me a hug that nearly breaks my spine. "Are you sure?" she says. "I mean, sure it'll suck for me to have to go to court, but that's me telling the truth. You making stuff up to get my uncle to admit what he did . . . that's crazy. Are you sure you'll be able to do that? What about the hives?"

"They're not literal hives, silly, like bees buzzing," I say lamely, like I'm not scared outta my socks. "He can't hear them forming over the phone." *I hope.*

The room buzzes with electricity. "Oooh," says Uncle Pasta. "I don't know how your daddy is going to feel about this, little girl."

"You let me handle her daddy," Mom answers.

I jump out of the chair and run over to where she sits on the couch, plopping between her and my uncle, hugging her fiercely. I'm terrified, but also buzzing and electric, like the room. "When do we want to make this call?" I ask. *Please, not today. I need some time to prepare.*

Tom says, "I think you and I need to hunker down in that office yonder and go through all the factors you'll need to consider when making the call. You can spend Tuesday preparing. . . ."

"*After* you go to school," Mom says.

I nod, knowing better than to start that fight again.

"You can spend all evening practicing."

"I'll make sure Lucas Perkins is at his hotel to answer the phone on Wednesday," continues Officer Lenox. "Does that sound like enough time? He seems to be sticking around here like we've told him to, for now, but if he starts gettin' squirrelly we're goin' to have to arrest him, and then I'm not sure if the plan will work."

I breathe deeply again, reaching for the last of the vanishing oxygen as I burrow in between Mom and Uncle Pasta. "OK, Wednesday. Let's write a script today, and tomorrow at school I have a plan—someone who can help me prepare."

Cora snaps to attention, "Oooh, is it Larson?" Her eyebrows are poised to do the Groucho Marx lift, but then she pauses. "Do you trust him not to go babbling to everyone at school? Not that I care, really. I'm sure they're all talking and making stuff up about me as it is, but . . ."

I shake my head. "No, it's not Larson. We'll talk about Larson later." *And how my fantasies about him have all been stomped to death by the boot of reality.* But that's OK. "It is someone I trust, although I'm not sure why, exactly. I'll tell you more about *that* later, too."

"All right, then," smiles Cora. It's a real smile, too, one I haven't seen since school started. She claps her hands together. "Let's go, chickadee! Let's save the day!" and everyone applauds, caught up in the excitement of the moment, as I try to ignore the taste of copper invading my mouth.

My hell, what have I gotten myself into?

ගගග

The courtyard at Pinewood High looks relatively empty at 6:45 Tuesday morning, just as it had at 6:45 Monday morning.

I recognize one of those couples who come to school early

so they can make out with each other against parent wishes, sitting on a concrete bench doing just that, while sharing earbuds. The headphone cords bind them, but not as well as the grasping hands or the entwined tongues. *Gross. I'm really not a fan of public displays of affection. I don't know if that makes me a prude or . . . a nerd with discriminating taste?*

Two gesticulating girls in berets, who obviously take their French class *very* seriously, are in the corner of the courtyard by the foreign language classrooms.

Cade Castell lounges against the oak tree by the auditorium, reading a comic book. *Tales from the Crypt*, I notice. Interesting.

I stroll up to Cade and plop down, leaning into the tree next to him. "Do you know where you came from?"

"Do you mean literally or figuratively?" He looks up from his comic, right at me.

I adjust my shoulder blades so the tree doesn't feel so pokey. "Well, so stated, the question leads to a whole myriad of possibilities, I can see. Someday I'll tell you why I say that. I mean literally."

He closes the book to give me all his attention. "Street, state, or country?"

"Country. You know, your ethnic background. What is Castell?"

"Spanish. Actually, it stands for Castillo, which in old-timey Spanish means 'castle worker' or 'dweller in a castle.' I choose to believe the second definition, because we're more likely to be ancient Spanish royalty if we actually dwelt in the castle, as opposed to building it."

Thank God. That is all I can think and I don't know why his answer makes me happy. *Why should I care if this guy knows his ethnic background or not?* "Why is it Castell now?"

"Aw, my dad is Basque." He drops the comic on the ground in front of his crossed legs and cranks around to face me, resting his shoulder on the tree instead of his back. "That's a Spanish group that lives in the Pyrenees. Apparently very traditional, old school, hardline, whatever. Anyway, *his* dad was a straight-off-the-boat Basque, who I guess pretty regularly beat the shit out of my dad. So my dad changed our name to Castell—I don't know if it was to wash his hands of my grandfather, or what."

"Would you rather have Castillo back?" I ask. "Sounds sort of dashing, very Don Juan."

He smiles, and I notice for the first time how nice his smile is. Very Colgate-toothpaste-commercial white and straight. *Why haven't I ever looked at his smile? This guy's been around me since the dawn of time.*

He drawls, "I'd rather my dad didn't get the shit beat out of him."

I nod. "*Touché.*"

I sit cross-legged to face him, take a deep breath, and dive in. "Cade, I need your help, and I need to trust you with some information that needs to stay with you, and then I need to rehearse it. I don't think I'm a very good actress, but this could be my most important role ever. Will you help me?"

Cade looks at me. Then he leans over and grasps both my hands in his. This close, I notice the lashes that border his dark blue eyes are about twelve miles long. *Wow.*

"Have you ever noticed," he wonders, "through all the years we've gone to school together, that sometimes we seem to share some sort of a look? A look that says, 'We're in . . .'"

I join him, "'We're in this together!'?" I nod. "I've noticed."

He squeezes my hands and then lets go. "I think we are, or we could be. So yes, you can trust me. And yes, I will help you. We're in this nuthouse—otherwise known as school—together."

Again: thank God.

I pull the RMCFC paperwork from my backpack. "OK, great. Hopefully Miss Bakener will give us some time to go over this in class. But we have a half-hour or so now, so let's talk about my friend Cora and what kind of acting skills you're going to have to help me pull right out my butt to save her. . . ."

28. Trepidation

trepidation /trepə 'dāSH (ə)n/ n. a feeling of fear or agitation about something that may happen.

🌀🌀🌀

"Hello?"

"Hello, this is Harper Southwood. May I please speak to Cade Castell?"

"This is he. Are you ready?"

"I don't know, Cade. I'm freaking out a little. No, I take that back. I'm freaking out a *lot*. My head feels like it's about to fall off my neck and roll out the door. Or maybe it will stay attached and then—BOOM!—just explode right here and now, on this very spot. I don't know if I can do this."

I sit in my room trying to gain courage from Cade's comforting voice, waiting for Officer Tom, who's going to come in and set up the recording equipment; also they want a witness to be in the room—I guess to make sure I call the right number. To back up the words the judge would hopefully hear on the recording. Possibly to make sure nothing blows up.

I have banished everyone else from the area, because I don't feel I can act in front of them all. I'm not even sure I can do it in front of Officer Tom.

"OK, breathe," says Cade. "You can do this. Remember, that police officer said the guy's a total narcissist. And we know he's a pedophile. Use what you know and play to his weaknesses. Swallow the puke that comes up in your throat at the thought of what he did to Cora, and pretend you're on another planet where that stuff is the norm. Then crucify him."

God, I can't believe there would be any planet that awful.

"He's here, Cade. Officer Tom is here. I can hear him coming up the stairs."

"You can do this, Harper. Give him your best magic mojo."

How does he know about my wish for supernatural mojo? I may just love him.

"I'll be thinking about you," he says. "I'll tell Miss Bakener not to worry about your absence, that you're doing her proud. Go to it!" Click.

Oh, God. Here we go.

ⓞⓞⓞ

A knock at the door.

"Miss Harper! You ready?" Good ol' boy Tom walks in the door to my room, in T-shirt and jeans. In cowboy boots, no less. He starts unpacking a large box on my bed.

"One of our on-duty officers just called me. He's been surveilling Lucas Perkins, and he confirmed that the man is home right now. Said he saw him bring a six-pack of beer in." He looks at his watch. "Well, I guess if he's drinkin' beer at seven a.m., that's good for us. Maybe he'll get good and tanked and start spittin' out all the incriminatin' evidence we need."

"Yeah," I say. "That would be mighty nice now, wouldn't it?"

Whoa. Where did that Southern belle sound come from?

"I do believe you've adopted my accent, Miss Harper. Is that *Gone with the Wind* talk part of your plan for the pretext call?"

"Naw, I don't even know where it came from. Do you think I should use an accent?" The words sugarcoat my tongue. *This is kinda interestin'. I wonder why I can do this? Maybe I really should start taking acting more seriously. Or maybe I should move to Nashville and start eating collard greens and grits with the rest of the population.*

He sits on my olive-green bedspread and picks up my ancient cordless phone. He starts attaching wiry sticky things to it, and it takes him over an hour to attach everything, to test it and retest it.

While he works, I practice lilting and twanging: I picture myself very Scarlett O'Hara, perched on the patio (I think Southern belles say *verandah*) drinking mint juleps and being wooed by scores of suitors. I'm not sure if I can pretend that this twisto is one of my suitors, but . . .

Finally, he places what looks like an iPod earbud inside his ear. "I don't know why people like the accent so much," he comments. "I think it soothes them. You're doing real well with it. You've never talked to him before, have you?"

I shake my head.

"Well, you do whatever you feel is best. I think you're very brave—did I tell you that?" His words come out "Ah think you're vehrry brayve."

I don't think the accent is soothing so much as it's very sexy. Maybe if I sound sexy for this sicko, he'll say what I need him to say.

I think of the words Cade and I had practiced, and in this moment, with the soothing-sexy Southern twang floating around the room, my original plan sounds too aggressive. Too tell-me-what-you-know-or-I'll-kill-you, and I all of a sudden know it won't work with Lucas Perkins. I do, indeed, have to swallow some barf that comes up my throat when I think about this new —and unrehearsed!—plan, but I also know that it's what will work.

"Officer Lenox?"

"Harper, I'm not one of your teachers. You may call me Tom."

I swallow spit. "Tom, I'm going to keep the accent and try to butter him up, I guess, to get him to talk. It's not what I practiced with my friend yesterday, but I feel like it's the right way to approach him. Do you think that will be OK?"

He places his hands on his knees. "Do you think it will work better than what you practiced?"

I nod. "I do. Ah really do." I mentally check myself, on the verandah with a mint julep. *Batting my eyelashes even though he can't see me. Palm to my chest, then swooning against the chair back. "Oh mah goodness, Mistah Perkins. The things you say!"* Gah.

"Hand me that phone number, would you, please? Thank you kindly, Tom." *There, sugar and molasses and maple syrup. I can't get any sweeter. Let's do this.*

He passes me the paper with the number, and pretends not to notice my shaking hands as I dial.

"Yeah?" The voice is scratchy, a cigarette smoker's voice although I assume Lucas Perkins can't smoke and body-build at the same time. Although what do I know? As the world is proving to me daily, the answer is: nothing.

"Lucas Perkins? Am Ah speakin' to Lucas Perkins?"

"Yeah?" Now the voice is cautious.

Here we go.

I pour it on. "Mistah Perkins, Ah'm Harper Southwood. Ah'm Cora's friend, but please, *please* don't tell her I'm calling you right now. Ah would simply die if she found out I was callin'. She'd be so vehry upset with me, thinkin' Ah'm buttin' my nose in what's none o' my business an' all. Y'all know how some girls can git, don'tcha now? Can y'all keep this vehry important secret for me, Mr. Perkins?"

There is a long pause. I wonder if he hung up. "Mistah Perkins?"

"Yeah, I'm here." I hear the crumple of aluminum, then a clink as it hits the wall—*aiming across the room at the trash can? You missed, asshole.* "What kinda secret could you have that I'd wanna hear about?"

His voice grates across the lines, and I feel a lightning bolt of pain fire between my shoulder blades.

What is that? Tom shoots a concerned look my way.

I arch my back and try to wiggle the pain out, then take a deep breath and plunge on, ignoring it. "I just—Ah'm just feelin' bad for you, Mistah Perkins. Everyone's sayin' all these horrible things about you, and I saw you at the hospital, and you looked so strong and big and muscular and *concerned.* You looked so concerned about Cora." I close my eyes. I don't know if I can do this. *Come on, Harper. You can do this.*

I can almost see him flexing and nodding his head. "I was. I am concerned about Cora. She's my niece, ya know, and I'm only here to help her and my brother." He burps, and I wait for the "excuse me." Nope.

"Like you did when her momma had cancer?" *When her mom had cancer, you jackass. Who does that? Who can do any of that?* I want to scream out loud, but instead I just keep swallowing air and trying to maintain my accent.

Officer Lenox watches me warily.

"Yeah, like that. I was only tryin' to help her." I hear the *chuff* of the pop-top as he opens another can and the *glurg* of a big swallow.

Yeah, keep drinking. Go ahead, choke on it.

"She needed someone, ya know? And my brother was so

busy freakin' out about his wife, he never had no time to pay attention to Cora."

OK, careful. Tread carefully. "Ah know, Ah know, Mr. Perkins! She told me all about how you two were superheroes fightin' to save her momma, and how you made her feel like y'all could use your combined superpowers to save her. Ah think she was vehry grateful to you for that." My back burns like fire.

His voice on the line sounds like a peacock in full preen. "She shoulda been. That was a big-time distraction, us being the superheroes. It made her feel like she had some power to deal with her mom's cancer. I've gotta say, it was a great idea, those superheroes."

OK, where do I go from here? Be careful, Harper. "And, when you touched her—did that help her deal with her momma's illness?"

He starts to object, but I keep on. "Ah mean, you are so strong—so handsome and strong. She probably felt comforted when those strong hands touched her, didn't she?"

I shiver, and the knife sitting between my shoulder blades twists and arcs. *Where is that pain coming from?*

Officer Lenox's—Tom's—hand covers his mouth as my body jerks, and he looks ready to jump across the bed and slam the phone into its cradle.

I shake my head and hold out a hand to stop him. *Don't.*

He clenches his fists and remains still, but I can see it's an effort.

"Mistah Perkins, please, please promise me you won't say nothin' to Cora 'bout this phone call. If she found out I was . . ." My cheeks puff out as air blows through them. I'm trying so hard not to throw up it makes my eyes water. "Was attracted to you. She'd nevah forgive me. I think she probably wants y'all to herself, and she must be sayin' all these things to hide her secret feelings. Don't you think?"

I hear the crumpling can. *Again?*

"She used to tell me she loved me all the time," he says. "I don't know why she stopped. Maybe my brother was getting superstitious."

Don't you mean 'suspicious,' you chowderhead? Suddenly I know, I know this is going to work. I wait for Lucas Perkins's response.

"Yeah. She loved me," he says finally. "She loved me and she wanted my help."

I suck in a huge breath. "So it was really no big thang, was it, Mistah Perkins, when you loved her *all the way*. She wanted your penis inside of her to make her feel that superhero strength, didn't she, Mistah Perkins? She wanted it? I imagine Ah would." I clap my hand over my mouth.

Tom's eyes are wide as dinner plates, but still he holds himself in check.

We wait.

"What are you talking about?" he says. "I thought you said you felt bad about the things people were saying."

I jump in. *No turning back now. No throwing up.* "I did. Ummm . . . Ah said Ah felt bad about the horrible things they were saying. Lahk you're a monster and other horrible things. Ummm . . . Ah think you needed to use any means you could to take Cora's mind off her momma. And you're so strong, lahk I said. So handsome and strong and virile. Sometimes sex is a great way to take people's minds off bad things, don'tcha think? And just because Cora was a little young. Still, if being with, ah . . . someone such as yourself could help her feel strong as well, and able to fight to save her momma." *Is there any way he could buy this? How could anyone believe this load of crap? Take another drink, please, Lucas.*

He did and followed that with a belch. And then, "Yeah, she was a little young when her mom died." His voice warms to the load of baloney I'm spoon feeding him. "I think that made her older. Yeah, she seemed a lot older, from dealing with her mom being sick, I bet. She was like a *reglar* young woman, like a woman inside of a little girl's body."

Sicko gag vomit ugh! "And so you treated her like a regular young woman, right?"

From the other end of the line I can hear a noise, a grunting sound like someone doing a massive stretch of satisfaction. *Like someone does when he's patting himself on the back.*

"Yeah," he says finally. "She wanted it. She pretended not to, but I know she wanted it. I loved her all the way."

I stare at Tom.

I don't know if that's enough, he mouths.

Eeuw gross this is so gross this is so gross disgusting gross sick puke. Not enough. God save us all, this better be enough.

"All the way," I repeat, "with your penis inside her?"

"Yeah, that too," he chuckles. "How else is she going to know how big my superhero powers are? She needed a real sample. She loved it. I don't know why she's going all crazy now. Just to piss us off, I think. Teenagers can be such a pain in the ass."

Tom Lenox bounces on my bed, nodding and pumping his fist to the sky. *You got it!* he mouths. *That's enough to get him.*

"Well, Ah'm sure sorry you feel that way, Mistah Perkins. Because I'm a teenager, you know."

"I guess you are," he says. "That's too bad. You sound younger. Do you look younger? Hey, what's the secret you were gonna tell me? I ain't heard no secrets yet."

I glance over at Tom, who's still bouncing on my girly bedspread. Teal and purple throw pillows shake and roll off the bed.

I mouth, *Are you sure that's enough?*

He nods. *Cut him loose,* he mouths through a wide smile.

"Well, yes, Mistah Perkins. Sorry, I forgot about the secret. You're goin' to love it. The secret is. . ." I wait.

"Yeah? What is it? Tell me."

I drop the accent. "I guess it's no real secret, *Lucas*. The secret is, the *truth* is, you are a narcissistic, solipsistic, self-aggrandizing, sociopathic bastard of a pedophile who wouldn't know heroism or compassion if it bit you in the butt and shoved you off the dock. You are one twisted sicko who has hurt my friend, my dear friend, one of the best people I know, and I hope you rot in hell for that. You *are* going to rot in JAIL, if I have anything to say about it."

I look at the hand not holding the phone. It's still shaking from the adrenaline. I smile at Officer Tom.

"And the great part about it is . . . I think I just did. I think I very much had something to say about it, and you just remember when you're staring at the empty walls of your jail cell and fending off the guys who are gonna eat you for breakfast, you kiddy molester, remember it was a pain-in-the-ass TEENAGER who put you there!"

That's for you, Cora. And with that, I place my older-than-dinosaurs cordless telephone into its cradle with a flourish.

And Officer Tom Lenox and I cheer, scream, and raise such a fuss that Uncle Pasta and Charles pour through the door in alarm.

29. SuCCeSS

success /sək'ses/ n. the accomplishment of an aim or purpose.

◉◉◉

"Oh, mah goodness!" I fan myself, the adrenaline still rushing through my bloodstream. "Ah don't think I can stand the excitement." I throw the rest of the decorative pillows off the bed and crash backward into it, barely rescuing the cordless phone and all the recording paraphernalia from tumbling overboard.

"Bella, my bella," says Uncle Pasta, plopping down next to me, "I take it your pretext call went a-well. And what is up wis zis new accent? You are trying to imitate ze police a-officer, no?"

"What happened, Harper? Did you get what you needed to put the bad man away?" asks Charles. "It certainly sounds like a success party in here."

"Oh, man." Tom sits down at my desk. "You shoulda *seen* this girl in action. She ups and dons this Scarlett O'Hara persona, and uses it to seduce Lucas Perkins into admitting he molested Cora—he actually sounded proud of it—and then once we had it on tape, she lays into him." He places his hands on his hips and starts wagging his finger at Charles and my uncle, speaking in a girly tone. *Do I really sound that goofy?* "You are a narcissistic, sociopathic, solip . . . solip *what?* I don't know that word, but it sure sounds rotten."

Uncle Pasta claps his hands. "Solipsistic? You used the word 'solipsistic'? That's one of my favorite words, bella!"

My face flushes with pride. No hives, I can just feel the apple-red in my cheeks. "I know, me too. I don't know how I came up with it, but it felt so terrific to tell him off. Even if it was in a language his Neanderthal brain couldn't comprehend."

And Cora, I can't wait to tell you what happened. If I ever had any desire to text, I would text an entire novel to Cora. I'll just call her at the hospital.

"Solipsism is the philosophical theory that the self is all that you know to exist," says Charles, "so . . ."

"So if the self is all you know exists, then nothing else matters," finishes Uncle Pasta. "The whole world revolves around you, because you are all that is, you know?"

"Well, I think a whole world of criminals is going to be revolving around Lucas Perkins pretty soon, here," I say, grinning like a Cheshire kitty. I rub my back. "Hey, Tom. My back feels better. That pain in my back is gone. Do you think it was just the stress of the call?"

"I wish I knew, but I'm glad you feel better. You did great, girl." Tom gathers the recording equipment, wrapping cords, disconnecting some pieces and clicking others together. "Wait till I tell Louisa, right after I call the judge for an arrest warrant. Speaking of people I need to tell, I can't wait to call Lucas Perkins's lawyer. I bet he scrambles to plea-bargain his client quicker'n grass through a goose, once he hears the tape. Gotta go." He stands up to give me a big hug, and waves to the group on his way out.

"What pain are we talking about, bella?"

"I don't know," I stretch my arms up above my head. "He started talking and all of a sudden a lightning bolt of pain struck right between my shoulder blades. Officer Tom almost hung up the phone when he saw my face." I shrug. "But it's gone now."

Charles sits down in the chair Officer Lenox vacated. "Do you think it is a 'troll power'?"

"What, that I sensed his sickness in my *back*?"

"Why not?" asks Uncle Pasta. "You sensed Cora's depression in your knees, right? Why not Lucas Perkins's mental illness in your back?" He picks up purple and teal pillows from the floor and lifts them up to my ears, holding my head.

I sigh. "I guess. It still seems so useless. Why sneeze? Why twitch my knees? Why sharp pain in my back? If I can't relate it to something specific that's going on, I can't help anyone. And then there's my mom—the one person I should have sensed something about, the one who is the most important to me and who has a serious chronic illness, and I've got bupkus. Some great party-conversation trick about worthless crap."

"I have a theory about that, actually." Charles squeezes in between me and Uncle Pasta on the bed. We line the front, facing the poster of the little boat in the Thai ocean, and I remember what Cora had said about falling off the edge of the world. *She almost did. I'm so glad she didn't.* "Do you want to hear it?" he asks.

"Sure, lay it on me, Charles," I say. "So far, I think you're pretty smart, so . . ."

He tickles me. "So far? SO FAR!" he roars. I push against Uncle Pasta to get away. "Wait until you hear my very educational treatise on why you should ditch the beautiful dumb jock and go for the intelligent and imaginative guy you never looked twice at."

And still he keeps tickling, as I writhe and giggle. "I might be way ahead of you on that one," I say. "*Uncle* Charles."

He stops tickling, and looks over me to smile at my uncle. My uncle grins back. They look so happy.

"Anyway. Here's my theory: autoimmune diseases don't involve any external or foreign invaders working their way into the body, right? Not caused by a germ or a virus or a chemical imbalance that didn't exist previously."

I nod. "Right. It's Mom's body fighting itself."

"So, maybe your gift can only detect those outside forces. Maybe it just didn't recognize something that was a part of her already."

I lie back down to digest this. "Hm. Maybe so. That sucks, though. And, like I said, none of it does anyone any good."

Uncle Pasta lies down next to me and clasps my hand. "It doesn't matter, bella. You are useful. You just saved Cora from publicly describing the worst experiences in her life, having to rehash a very private horror in front of a very public courtroom. You are a fabulous rock for your mother, and she depends on you for love and support. You are one of the kindest, most caring, wonderful people I know, and *those* are your gifts. Those are the only ones that matter."

I throw my arm across his chest. "Thanks, Uncle Peter. I think you have all those gifts, too, in spades. Speaking of my mother, where is she?"

"Your dad took her to the acupuncturist." He looks at his watch. "She should be home right about . . ."

"Now!" says Mom from the doorway. "I sent your dad to work. I'm feeling pretty good." She moves slowly, yet perkily, to my desk chair. "I like acupuncture needles much better than the needles I have to shove into rotating spots on my body, that's for sure. Acupuncture needles don't hurt at all; as a matter of fact, I fell asleep on the table, with some sticking out of my legs, my wrists, and one smack in between my eyes."

"Ah, ancient Chinese medicine," quips Charles. "Four thousand years' worth of billions of Chinese people can't be wrong."

"Is your acupuncturist from China?" asks Uncle Pasta.

Mom starts her finger counting exercise again. "No, interestingly enough, she's a redheaded Coloradan." She chuckles. "Very well trained, though, right here in America. I know she's done a lot of training in China, too. They think she's evil and scary there, apparently. I loved her."

"Wait, wait," I say. "They think she's scary because she's a redhead? I've heard that blondes garner a lot of attention in China, but . . ."

"No, no, that's what I thought," Mom says. "It's because she's left handed. They don't like us southpaws in China. I guess they didn't pay the slightest attention to her red hair until she picked up a pen. Anyway, she's great. She learned a lot about me, and I think she's going to do so much to help with the MS. It's all about balance, ya know? The Chinese don't see the body in the same way we Westerners do, all technical and autopsied and 'treat the symptoms after they come.' They treat the whole body as a series of systems that flow and fly in a certain way. Disease is just like the word sounds—the system is in *dis-ease*, and restoring the balance eliminates the *dis-ease*."

"Makes us easy, so to speak?" asks Charles. He starts singing the Eagles, "Take it Easy," and Mom and Uncle Pasta shimmy their shoulders in time.

Everyone around me is a total goofball. I love it so much. We put the fun in functional, really we do. I guess I'm getting over the troll thing, but if I really were a troll who got dropped into this family, I'm wicked grateful for the switch.

"The Chinese have a totally different view of the human body," continues Mom. "They don't believe in autopsies—so Harper, you wouldn't have to worry about cat dissection in China —but they see all these meridians running through each of us. Keep the meridians clear and running smoothly, and the body remains healthy. The weird thing is, the needles don't get placed in the part where the pain or the disease is located, necessarily, but in the best part of the meridian, so the flow of *qi*—pronounced 'Chee'—keeps on uninterrupted."

Mom swishes her hands across her arms, presumably showing some places where the *qi* can flow. "I'll tell you, Charles, Sara told me placing needles inside your *ear* can work to control your blood sugar. Weird, huh?"

She stops, and looks at me. "Silly me, I'm so wrapped up in my own *qi*, I forgot why I came in here. What happened with the call to Lucas Perkins?" She looks around. "I see Officer Lenox has gone. Did it go OK? Come on, spill!"

Charles and Uncle Pasta start tripping over each other to sing my praises, but I am struck by Mom's words: *you use an acupuncture needle in the EAR to treat diabetes*. I wonder. . .

I hop up and walk over to my computer desk. I gingerly (but perkily) move my mom over to the bed, move myself back, and sit down at the keyboard. "You guys go right ahead and keep paying homage to me. I've got to look something up."

30. Relief

relief /rəˈlēf/ n. a feeling of reassurance and relaxation following release from anxiety or stress.

⟡⟡⟡

Thursday morning and it's the Cleaver household all over again. I wake to sunlight peeking through the slats in my blinds and birds singing from the trees I can see out my window, and when I head downstairs, my whole family's sitting at the table, ready to send me off to school with a tummy full of breakfast (courtesy of my father) and cheeks full of kisses (courtesy of my mother and uncle).

I still don't know how everything's going to turn out with the pretext call and with my mom's MS, but the world seems more like a place I can inhabit today. More like a place I can belong and contribute to—troll or teenager, useless curse or helpful gift.

Cade's in what I've come to think of as his "usual place," even though we've only been in school two-ish weeks and I've only seen him there two-ish times. This time, though, instead of his usual lounging position against the back of the big old tree, he almost seems perched, sitting up straight and . . . *waiting for me?*

Oh yeah, I didn't call him last night about the pretext call. He's waiting to hear about that, I'm sure. But still, he smiles that toothpaste grin through all the piercings, and he looks happy to see me, and I feel a strange flicker in my stomach. *What is THAT all about?*

I plop down next to the tree. Next to Cade.

"Hey! I didn't hear from you last night about the phone call," he says. "How'd it go? Did you punch that predator's clock? I sat and wondered about the approach we'd practiced all night, and thought about narcissism, and read some more about it, and I sort of worried that we'd . . ."

"That we'd practiced the wrong approach?"

He nods.

"Well, that occurred to me, too. So I latched onto the police officer's Southern accent and I seduced the molester. I seduced that monster over the phone—it almost made me barf, but I did —and I got him to admit what he did to Cora."

Cade's eyebrows shoot up, and the ring in his brow quivers. "He admitted it straight out? That's fantastic!" He holds up his hand for the high-five. "So, when do you find out if he took a plea bargain? Wow, that's so cool. You must feel awesome, like the superhero badass we practiced, only . . . sweeter."

I throw on the accent for Cade. "Sure, sugah-pie-honey-bun, Ah am sweeter than a self-eatin' watermelon, don'tcha know?"

His grin about splits his face in two. "Well, ma'am, if I didn't know before, Ah am sure fixin' to now!"

And we laugh and laugh, and it's suddenly an even better day than it had been before.

I think about my research from last night. "Hey, remember on our get-to-know-you day, how I told you about my body doing all these weird things around people getting sick?"

He nods. "Like you sneeze or your nose twitches or whatever when someone's getting a cold or flu?"

"Right, right." I pat him on the knee, then have to make a conscious effort to pull my hand off of his leg. *Oops.* "Well, when I was in the middle of the pretext call yesterday, I had this shooting pain right between my shoulder blades."

"Hey, we know that guy is sick, right? Twisted sick, but . . ."

"Yup, yup but wait, there's more. So my uncle's boyfriend is a diabetic, right? And I didn't know this, so I came down for breakfast the other day and he's giving himself insulin shots. And I had this stinging pain in my *ear*, of all places."

He stares at me. "That doesn't seem related to anything. Insulin production is in the pancreas."

Now I pound on his leg. "Exactly! That's the whole problem. But then my mom, my mom went to the acupuncturist and learned some stuff about acupuncture."

He grins again, "Like, billions of Chinese for the past four thousand years have to be doing something right?"

"Ooh, Mistah Castell. You are smarter than a pig in a poke, bless your heart."

The first bell rings, and Cade helps me up as we walk toward the auditorium. "Hmmm. And a poke is a smart place to be, for a pig, I guess?"

I giggle. *Look at me, giggling like a schoolgirl in front of this scary Goth guy. I guess I AM technically a schoolgirl, but . . .* "I don't know, I just heard that somewhere. I suppose a poke could actually be a dumb place for a pig, but I like the alliteration."

We cross the open doors of the auditorium, and kids are already on the stage.

"So, anyway, last night I looked up all this information on acupuncture. And I found out that these places I've been feeling pains or twitches or whatever, they relate to the places the

Chinese feel you need to control to deal with those illnesses. Chinese medicine treats diabetics with acupuncture needles placed in the inside of the ear, exactly where I felt the pain when I saw my uncle's boyfriend." *This sounds crazy, I know, but crazy in a possibly useful sort of way.*

Cade's nodding at me to continue, so I do.

"Like I looked up the spot where I had the pain in my back. It's a channel called DU-12, and I don't really understand the stuff yet, but there're all these pathways in your body, and acupuncturists help clear blockages in the pathways, hence cure illnesses in the body associated with the blockage."

Miss Bakener pushes through the group of students who are fooling around on the stage. Her broomstick skirt is especially colorful this morning and she swishes it back and forth as she crosses, almost sweeping the students off the stage.

"Take your seats, actors! Today we are practicing stage combat and other techniques for feigning realism in front of an audience."

The students on stage cheer. "So anyway," I say, as we traipse down the theater aisle to our seats, "DU-12 is some sort of channel that relates to anger—a 'rage with desire to kill' to be exact."

"No kidding. And what about the knee twitching thing with Cora?"

"Oh, that part's *waay* interesting. There are two spots that correspond with the place I felt the twitching: GB-34 and ST-36. Again, I don't know what all the points mean, yet, but those two have to do with fear and fright and manic depression! Isn't that a trip?"

"Actors! Give me your attention," Miss Bakener calls. "You and your partner are going to learn how to eat, use the phone, shoot, stab, punch, rack your partner . . . that's my favorite, and kiss, which *would* be my favorite if the principal actually let you do that the way it should be done. So grab yourself a partner and here we go!"

"Yes, that is the trippiest," Cade agrees. He stands and starts to lead me out of the row and up to the stage, which I assume means we're going to be partners.

That's fine with me. Maybe better than fine.

"You know, it sounds to me like you're an empath of some sort," he says. "You know, like you can feel other people's pain or angst like it's your own, only in this case it's other people's illnesses. I don't know. Maybe I'll have to look it up."

He continues dragging me up the stairs to the stage, and all I can think is *HE's going to have to LOOK something UP? Yes, this is better than fine. It's fabulous.*

"OK, one more time, people!" calls Miss Bakener. "Clint and Preston, especially." She's referring to these two football players, one of whom is still lying on the stage holding his crotch. "When you do a *stage* rack, you knee your partner on the *inner thigh*, not on the actual privates themselves. That's dangerous. See, Clint, look at Preston. He's down for the count." She throws up her hands in frustration, and Cade and I try so hard not to laugh out loud at Preston as he writhes on the floor.

Don't break character, class. Keep your composure! Even when your blockheaded friend knocks you almost unconscious with pain.

Miss Bakener wipes her hands like she's cleansing herself of Clint and Preston's stupidity. "OK, let's try our last stage action: kissing. As I said before, when actors are on stage, on a real Broadway stage, they have to actually kiss their partners. It's not that big of a deal, people, it's lips touching lips. It's called acting. But like I said, the principal won't let me teach that stuff. Maybe he thinks it will lead to sex off the stage, I don't know. Anyway, there are two ways to stage kiss without actually touching anyone's lips."

She continues by showing us a sort of ballroom dip, where

the kisser's head covers the kissee's head at the bottom of the dip, so all the audience sees is the back of the kisser's head and the kissee's forehead, hopefully with eyes closed and eyebrows raised so it looks like the couple is enjoying it.

Then all the girls have to sit on a chair facing the audience to receive a fake kiss. She makes the pairs with two guys do it too. I, personally, cannot imagine tromping up to some chair-sitter, remaining in a standing position and leaning over to passionately kiss him.

I guess if my dad were leaving for work and he just wanted a brief I'm-going-to-work kiss goodbye, but . . . No, it's just lame, either way. How many stage plays require a going-to-work kiss goodbye to move the plot forward? My guess is, none.

I guess the plot of the class needs to move forward, though, so I maneuver myself onto a chair facing the empty auditorium seats, and Cade stands in front of me. He takes one step to the side and leans from his waist. He unhooks his ponytail and makes his long, black hair cascade so his head and the fall of hair create a sort of wall.

He leans in and winks. "It's called acting, people." And he then proceeds to lay a complete, actual, lip-on-lip kiss right on me!

I'm stunned. His lips are soft, and he holds the kiss just long enough for me to close my eyes and raise my eyebrows, because, *ladies and gentlemen, I'm really enjoying it. Where on earth did that come from?*

I look around. No one else seems to notice me melting into the chair's surface, because Preston has just shoved Clint across the floor, shouting, "Get away from me, you asshole!"

"Homophobia has no place in the theater, people!" Miss Bakener shouts, and rushes through the pairs to try and keep a fight from breaking out. It takes about ten minutes for her to calm the class down and get us back to our chairs, and by then the bell rings.

"Tomorrow we start our first scenes with actual words, actors! Memorized words!" she says as we file out. "Come prepared to flex your acting muscles."

I walk out next to Cade, but I'm not sure what to say. *Did he kiss me just because that's the way the exercise was really supposed to go in real acting?* Maybe. But I don't think so. I think he couldn't care less how things were really supposed to go.

"Hey, Cade!" calls some Goth friend of his who's waiting for him outside the auditorium door. "We've got to get the shit ready to go for Armstrong's class."

He nods toward his friend. "Coming." He turns toward me and backs up in that direction, still looking at me. "Harper? Don't forget. We're in this together." And he turns and jogs away. Well, as much as you can jog through the minuscule openings left in the hallway by large packs of space-sucking students.

☉☉☉

I can't even remember what happened in PE or Algebra, except I think Ms. HAG-lione about popped an artery when that heavy girl, Allison, flat refused to climb that rope with the knots, saying something about how PE was the very definition of public humiliation and she was dropping the class and moving to Aerobics. *Good for you, Allison!*

Anyway, I spent those periods pondering soft lips and long, uncurly black hair.

My trancelike state is interrupted when I get to Anatomy. Larson McCready sits at our cat dissection table, and he gives me that crooked smile I'd been dreaming about for the past year and a half. *He's cute. Really cute. But worth a year and a half of my fantasy life? Not so sure.*

"Hey, Harper," he says. "We're all done with the dissection part of Spike. Now we have to do a writeup. I was hoping, since you've been, like, gone . . . you might think about . . ."

"I might think about doing the writeup?" I ask.

He shrugs, "Well, you know, it's just . . ."

"I know, I know. That's fair. I can do it tonight. Just give me your notes."

"Cool. You're the coolest. There's a football game tonight, ya know, and I'm needin' to go cheer on those Wildcats, ya know? I'd ask you to go, but you have to do the writeup, ya know? Hey, there's another game on Friday, do you want to go to that one?"

He cocks his head and raises one eyebrow, and all I could think was *this guy just said 'like' and 'ya know' way more times than is necessary for a single sentence, and I don't really care about his grammar. Not really, it's just . . .*

"You're *going* to the football game? I thought you were going to be the next John Elway. You mean you're *not* on the team?" I ask.

He gathers up the paperwork and slides it toward me. "Yeah, well, I *was* on the team as a freshman. Clint Dawson like, broke my collarbone in a practice and my mom told me I couldn't play again till college. I just said I was going to be as famous as John Elway, didn't I? Who knows, maybe I'll be a rock star. Hey, yeah, even more famous than John Elway. A rock star, I like that."

Or maybe you'll get a healthy dose of reality and maturity and find something productive to do with your life. Sure, I need to do that, too. I just don't think someone like Larson McCready is going to help me find a way to do it. "Sure, Larson. I like that. You could call your band Spike's House."

He looks intrigued. Holy Cow.

I shake my head to release my delusions about this boy. Hopefully for good. "Anyway, I'm just going to go find a desk over here to work on the writeup, if that's OK with you. Thanks for the game invite, though. Have fun!"

Wait a minute. Was that a date? Did Larson McCready just ask me for a date, or an opportunity to hang out with him, at least, and did I just turn him down? I think I did. And I think that's OK. I think I feel OK about it. As a matter of fact, I think I feel AMAZING about it. Wow. That is the craziest thing ever.

And I leave my dream man so he can play with some other pseudo-football-playing rock stars, and I leave Spike's dissection table while smiling like a live, undamaged cat who just swallowed a really tasty canary.

31. Purpose

purpose /ˈpərpəs/ n. the reason for which something is done or created or for which something exists.

ⓋⓄⓋ

I see the *tai chi* foursome on the road as I walk home. "Hi!" I say. "You're out late in the day, this time. Usually I see you in the morning."

They all smile, but it's the winking old guy who answers. "We just felt like switching it up. It only got up to eighty degrees today, so we're going to have to start going later. It's bound get too cold here pretty soon."

The lady preceding him chimes in, "Plus, pretty soon you might not even see us on this street any more. We're going to move our route over to Sparrow Street for a change of scenery."

The old guy says, "Yes, it's very nice to see your smiling face every morning on your way to school, and it's a beautiful street, but . . ."

"But it's getting boring," says the lady. "We've decided we need a street with more to it than just beauty. Maybe more twists and turns, more hills and valleys, more . . ."

"Challenges?" I say.

As they inch past me, this time it's the lady in the front who speaks. She's the shortest of the four and her gray hair is fluffed around her head in a senior-style Afro. "Right, honey. You know Sparrow is beautiful in its own right, although perhaps not in the traditional sense. But I think it'll be a fantastic street to get to know. I don't know why we never looked at it before . . . it's been right down the block forever."

"That's it," says the old guy. "We could really have a fantastic love affair with Sparrow Street. I can't wait. We'll miss you though, girlie."

I wave to the *tai chi* foursome as they trickle past. The metaphor doesn't escape me.

My house is occupied when I get there. I mean *really* occupied. Charles's car sits in the driveway next to Uncle Pasta's, and the curbs on either side of the driveway hold two unfamiliar sedans and a police car. *Officer Lenox?* And, *Ohmigod*, the Perkins Plumbing truck. *Are the police here to arrest my dad?*

I creep up the walk, fear building in my heart and hives growing on my neck. *Ohmigod. Are the plainclothes policemen here to take my dad to the slammer? I don't know if they put assault arrests into jails where they get instant boyfriends. Oh, jeez, he's fighting homophobia as it is.*

I stand paralyzed before the front door. *Let me think. What could I say to mitigate the situation? My mom has MS. We didn't know. My dad was just trying to protect his family and our friend. Don't arrest him, don't. . . .*

The door flies open. "Surprise!"

And Uncle Pasta reaches out, grabs me, and twirls me through the door. I come to a clumsy stop in front of a sea of smiling faces. Officer Lenox and Louisa Tripoli are here. Charles stands next to an older woman I've never seen before, beaming. Mom sits on the couch with Dad standing behind her, hands on her shoulders.

She's the only one seated, and I know she must be tired, or she'd have been at the door next to my uncle, pirouetting with us both.

And slightly to the left of Charles, looking wan and skinny, but for the first time in several weeks very happy, is my friend Cora.

"Cora!" I shout. "You're here! You're out of the hospital and you're here!" I run to her and hug her like a five-year-old who's found her lost Barbie. "Did my parents get you out? Did Officer Lenox? How do you feel? Oh, I've been thinking about you so much, I couldn't concentrate, I turned down a date with Larson, I got kissed. Oh, Cora, so much has happened I can't believe it. We have so much to talk about, my friend, and . . ."

I stop. I look around. The sea of faces stares at me, still happy but mostly amused. *I'm sure. I'm prattling on like a loony. What is happening? Why are all these people here?* "Officer Lenox? What's going on? Did I miss a birthday?"

Good ol' boy Tom steps forward and starts pumping my hand. "Harper, I heard from the lawyer. Lucas Perkins pled guilty to felony charges of 'sexual molestation of a minor while in a position of power.' He got twenty-five years. *Twenty-five years!*"

He's grinning like a demon. "His lawyer explained to him that the tape gave us enough to potentially put him away for life, plus I found an ex-girlfriend of his who has a daughter. When I approached the ex, she said she'd had her own suspicions about Lucas, and she'd talk to her daughter and see if she'd be willin' to find a counselor to talk about it. The lawyer mentioned the girlfriend to Lucas, explained the severity of what was on the tape, and he took the plea. You did such a great job, Harper. Everyone here is so proud of you."

The room breaks into applause. I look at Cora, and her eyes shine. *I did it for you*, my look says.

I know, says hers.

We hug again.

"So," I ask. "How did you get here, again?"

"My dad let me borrow the truck, believe it or not." She breaks into a whisper so the policeman can't hear. "I don't have my license yet, I know, I know. But he just handed me the keys and said, 'Go see your friend. Be careful.'" Her whisper turns throaty. "Last night he broke out the Candyland game from when I was five years old. We used to play it with mom. I'm not five, ya know, but he's, like, totally trying. 'S'nice, ya know?"

I'm so, so happy, we bump our two-thumbs-up symbols together and hug again, grinning like idiots. "I know. I know!"

She returns to a normal voice. "Hey, what do you call a missing parrot?"

I shake my head. "What?"

"A polygon. Get it, Polly's gone?" Her eyebrows shoot skyward. "Hey, did you say you turned down a date with Larson McCready?"

"I get it. Thanks. And yes, I did. I think it was a date, anyway. Maybe just a 'hang.' Whatever, I said no."

"Well," she smiles, "I didn't want to say anything, but I'm pretty sure that beautiful boy barely has two brain cells to rub together, am I right? You deserve so much better."

I do, don't I? "I do, don't I? No, he's really nice. But we have about as much in common as a pickle and a park bench." I stroke my chin like Sherlock Holmes. "Now, Cade Castell and I, we finish each other's sentences. And did I mention he kissed me?"

Cora's eyes bulge.

"Ahem." This from Uncle Pasta.

Cora and I come out of our trance. The sea of faces is still there, still looking amused, but . . . *Ohmigod, how rude are we?* I walk to Charles. "Hi, Charles. And this is?"

"This is my mother, Alicia Landover," says Charles, and I reach out to shake her hand.

Alicia Landover looks about fifty, with a curly blond bob that gives her a Shirley Temple look, or maybe it's the cupid's-bow lips. "Congratulations, Harper," she says. "Everyone here is very proud of you. Did you say someone named Cade kissed you? Well, I'm sure we all want to hear about *that*. And Charles says you have a special, four-thousand-year-old ability. I'm sure we all want to hear about that, too. Peter made cookies. And milk. We can all have a celebratory after-school snack and talk about it."

She takes my hand and leads me to the couch to sit next to Mom, who pulls me down and wraps me in a bear hug as the rest of the party looks for a place to sit and eat their cookies and milk.

"How's my beeyouteeful little girl?" Mom asks. Cora sits next to her on the couch's arm. "So Cora, do you know this Cade who's been kissing my beeyoutiful little girl?"

Cora nods. "I do, actually. He's really hot, in an alternative, vampire-boy sort of way. And he's wicked smart. I approve. Are you going to tell us where and why he was kissing you in the middle of the day?"

I think I changed my mind about telling people, actually. I just want to enjoy the possibilities of Cade without advertising it to a houseful of people. I'm opening my mouth to say so, when I feel a really strange combination of itching and burning in my upper arm.

Charles's mom says, "Harper, your phone is going to ring upstairs. I think you'd better go get it. I think it's important. Mr. Southwood, I think you'd better go, too."

Everyone in the room looks at her, noting the silence upstairs, except Charles, who nods and swishes his hand at me and my dad. I remember Charles's story about his mom and phones, and I'm for sure not going to question her gift when

I'm only beginning to figure out mine. I grab my dad away from the back of the couch and start dragging him up the stairs.

Maybe I could be a diagnostician of some sort. Or a psychiatrist. You know what's really cool? I'm starting to believe I can be anything I want, whether it utilizes some bizarre sense I don't really understand or not. Feels good.

My ancient phone jingles when we are halfway up the staircase.

"Hello?"

"Harper? It's Joseph Perkins. Can I talk to you for a second?"

Oh, wow.

My dad raises his eyebrows, a quizzical look on his face.

"Um, sure, Mr. Perkins. What's up?"

Dad and I share our ears to the phone as I rub my arm, up and down from shoulder to elbow. The burning and itching comes to a peak right in the middle.

I hear a deep, hesitant sigh on the other line. "I just . . . I just wanted to say I'm sorry. I know what my brother did to Cora. I know he did it, I knew even before he pled guilty. I just . . ." I hear a shuddering intake of breath. "I just thought it would be so much better if Cora was a troubled teenager, instead of my own brother being a—a monster. I didn't handle it good at all. When I think Cora is alive because of you and almost dead because of me, I . . ."

"Oh, no, Mr. Perkins. Don't say that."

"Well, it's true." His voice scratches the phone wires, and I know he's crying. "I used to be an OK dad. But I lost this beautiful woman who helped me be a better dad, and now I can't do shit and I almost killed my daughter. Hell, I even tried to kill *your* dad, and he's good at his job as a father. I should be shaking his hand, but now I'm too much of an idiot to even look at him. I don't . . ." he pauses. "I don't know what I'm saying. I just wanted to apologize and thank you for being there for Cora, and to tell you I hope—I hope . . ." he trails off.

"Mr. Perkins, hold on." I gesture the phone at Dad, who actually looks eager to talk to him. "I think my father would like to talk to you. He's not mad, really."

"Joseph? How're ya doing?" Dad booms, and then lowers his voice and walks into the hallway.

I take the opportunity to jump onto my computer and search through a new favorite file of mine, even though I know cookies are waiting downstairs.

He returns a couple of minutes later and sits on the bed. "That sounds great. . . . Yes, Cora will be fine here with us until the weekend. So I'll see you Saturday morning? . . . No, *ebel*—they're called *ebel-skeebers*. You and Cora are going to love them."

He clicks off and sighs a big sigh, talking to my back. "Harper. My girl, my daughter. You do know I love you, don't you?"

"I know, Daddy." *I know I am so happy to be a part of this family.* I press a key and step off my computer chair to snuggle down into his shoulder. The printer on my desk whirs and spits out a paper.

"You have many great gifts," he says to the top of my head. "And you're not a troll. You're a beautiful, wonderful girl, and I'm proud to know you are my flesh and blood. You know you are my flesh and blood, don't you?"

"Thanks, Daddy. Yes, I know. I don't really think I'm a troll anymore." I reach to pick up the paper from the computer. "I do think your flesh and blood has a cool superpower, though. Look at this." I show him an anatomical drawing of an arm. Black spots labeled about fifteen different areas of the arm, an anatomical connect-the-dots. I point to one. *LU-3: Sadness.*

"That's where your arm was hurting you, isn't it?"

I nod.

"You're right. That is a cool superpower. But your real superpower is your ability to care, and your mom and I are so glad you're using that ability to help us, and Cora, Peter, and Charles, through anything that comes our way." He squeezes me tight.

"And Cade?" I ask. "What if I want to showcase my caring abilities with a smart, sexy Goth guy named Cade?"

"We'll talk about that later. After I meet him, and decide whether or not I need to be cleaning my gun on the couch when he comes knocking at our door." He stands and pulls me toward the group downstairs. "Come on, let's have some cookies and milk."

Yes, let's.

Let's also take a look at Harper Southwood's blessings here on Glad Mountain Drive. . . . First, I'm so glad I'm not a troll. I'm so glad Cora's going to start working toward healing, both mentally and physically. And I'm so glad my mom can see and we can all do research on alternative ways to keep her healthy, and I'm so glad my uncle has found someone he loves and maybe can be with for a long time.

I'm just, overall, pretty glad to be me.

And I am EVER so glad, ecstatic really, that my dad doesn't actually own a gun.

thE End

Hotlines

If you see something, say something!

National Child Abuse Hotline:
1-800-4-a-Child (1-800-422-4453)

National Domestic Violence Hotline:
1-800-799-7233

Recipe

Ebel-Skeebers (Aebleskivers)

Notes:

Serve the warm pancake balls with butter and jam or dusted with powdered sugar. To make filled aebleskivers, add about 1/2 teaspoon jam to the batter in each cup just before you make the first turn. Serve the pancake balls as they are cooked, or keep warm in a napkin-lined basket until all are ready. The batter can also be cooked on a lightly buttered griddle over medium heat to make light, tender pancakes.

For mile-high baking, reduce the baking powder to 2 1/2 teaspoons.

Yield:
Makes 12 or 13 pancake balls

Ingredients:
- 1 1/4 cups all-purpose flour
- 3 tablespoons sugar
- 2 3/4 teaspoons baking powder
- 1/4 teaspoon ground cardamom or ground cinnamon
- 1/4 teaspoon salt
- 1 large egg
- 1 cup milk
- About 2 tablespoons melted butter or margarine

Preparation:
1. In a bowl, mix flour with sugar, baking powder, cardamom, and salt. In a small bowl, beat egg to blend with milk and 2 tablespoons butter. Add liquids to dry ingredients and stir until evenly moistened.

2. Place an aebleskiver pan over medium-low heat. When pan is hot enough to make a drop of water dance, brush pancake cups lightly with melted butter and fill each to slightly below the rim with batter.

3. In about 1 1/2 minutes, thin crusts will form on bottom of each ball (centers will still be wet); pierce the crust with a slender wood skewer and gently pull shell to rotate the pancake ball until about half the cooked portion is above the cup rim and uncooked batter flows down into cup. Cook until crust on bottom of ball is again firm enough to pierce, about another minute, then rotate ball with skewer until the ridge formed as the pancake first cooked is on top. Cook, turning occasionally with skewer, until balls are evenly browned and no longer moist in the center, another 10 to 12 minutes. Check by piercing center of last pancake ball added to pan with skewer—it should come out clean—or by breaking the ball open slightly; if balls start to get too brown, turn heat to low until they are cooked in the center. Lift cooked balls from pan and serve hot. Repeat to cook remaining batter.

Nutritional Information (per pancake ball):
    Calories: 88 (30% from fat)
    Protein: 2.3g
    Fat: 2.9g (sat. 1.6)
    Carbohydrate: 13g
    Fiber: 0.3g
    Sodium: 180mg
    Cholesterol: 24mg

Afterword

A recent study found that we are experiencing the highest recorded prevalence of mental illness in the US adolescent and young adult population.

    Ms. Bowles addresses this painful reality in the humor and pathos of her adolescent heroine, Harper.

    Queries, laughter, and tears embue this story about physical and mental illness and friendship and love. We journey with Harper through self-doubt and abuse to hope and inspiration. Readers will feel the laughter and tears of adolescence and will grow with the characters as they blossom and mature with courage, tolerance, and love.

    Bowles has the knack to delight and entertain while educating. Our youth and their parents will be amused and challenged in this belly of a whale.

—Kenneth A. Khoury, MD

Dr. Khoury is a practicing psychiatrist and a member of the American and the California Psychiatric Associations and was a past president of the San Diego Psychiatric Society and a former chair of the President's Committee of the San Diego Psychiatric Society. He was an assistant clinical professor of psychiatry at the University of California, San Diego, and served as the medical director of Scripps Behavioral Health Associates.

ACKNOWLEDGEMENTS

To Gerardeen Santiago, Daniel Primbs, and the staff at Aionios Books, my heartfelt thanks for your tireless work with and support of this book. I've felt from the beginning that your love for Harper and her story are EXACTLY what any writer wants in a publisher. It's beautiful inside and out. You rock!

Many thanks to Pete Hautzinger, the District Attorney for my hometown of Grand Junction, Colorado. His information on pretext calling and other legal elements of the story are much appreciated.

Thank you to Dr. Ken Khoury for looking at the book and at Harper from a cultural and social standpoint. As a writer, my main goals are to help my reader feel for the characters and situations, and escape into a different world, but I'd also like them to learn something, and your afterword helps frame this perspective. You are MY "Wonder Woman," too. :-)

To Richard Lai, you help keep me up to date on all the ways I'm researching to hone a worldview and a compassionate empathy for others. Thank you, my friend!

Ashley Giordano McKee, I needed you to write this book. You know what I'm talking about. I hope I did it justice. Thank you!

To everyone who gave their help and input to this book as it came together, from setting to character, sentence structure to cover art feedback, thank you! So many people are a part of the whole. Please don't be mad if I forgot you—just remind me REALLY LOUDLY so I can make sure to remember for every book from this moment forward. Keri Crovella, Leslie Anderson, Sara Beckner, Kim Orozco, Kirby Bowles, Cindi Pierce, and Wendy Urushima-Conn, thank you for being there for me.

Shawn Clingman, don't forget you are my superhuman superhero superstar. I need your help and feedback and aid, for this book and every book I will ever write from this moment forward. It's a big responsibility, I know. But I have complete faith in you.

To my mom and dad: Shelley and Don Bowles, you are an important part of everything I do and everything I have. Thank you! I love you so much.

Finally, to my family, Jim, Grey, and Griffen, thank you always. There can never be enough gratitude for the amazing life we're building together. I love you always, forever, and no matter what.

To anyone who's reading this book, thank you. I'm so excited to share Harper with you.

ABOUT THE AUTHOR

Kelley Bowles Gusich writes young adult fiction novels under the pen name Kelley Kay Bowles. Kelley taught high school English and drama for twenty years in Colorado and California, but a 1994 diagnosis of multiple sclerosis has brought her, circuitously and finally, to the life of writer and mother, both occupations she adores and dreamed about way back when she was making up stories revolving around her Barbie and Ken dolls. Her debut novel, cozy mystery *Death by Diploma* (under the pen name Kelley Kaye), was released by Red Adept Publishing, February 2016, and is first in her *Chalkboard Outlines®* series.

Kelley has two wonderful and funny sons and an amazing husband who cooks for her. She lives in Southern California.

To learn more about Kelley, visit her website and blog at www.kelleykaybowles.com.

Follow her on social media @kelkay1202. Post comments using #HarpersPower.

CPSIA information can be obtained
at www.ICGtesting.com
Printed in the USA
FSHW012014061218
54305FS